The True Self

The True Self

J.R. Singh

Writers Club Press
San Jose New York Lincoln Shanghai

The True Self

Writers Club Press
an imprint of iUniverse.com, Inc.

For information address:
iUniverse.com, Inc.
5220 S 16th, Ste. 200
Lincoln, NE 68512
www.iuniverse.com

ISBN: 0-595-19197-5

Printed in the United States of America

PREFACE

The True Self contains two inspiring stories which are a synthesis of fiction, mysticism, spiritual beliefs and some practical realities of life. It is hoped to be a life-long companion for those who seek a deeper understanding of the universe and the purpose of their lives. The events cited in this book dealing with matters of this life and the one hereafter are all worthy of deep reflection.

CRYONIC MAN

CHAPTER I

At 11:45 p.m. on a hot August night my drunken husband, Jim, began yelling for me to open the door. But on this night I decided not to let him into the house because I had grown tired of his rowdy behavior. He kept swearing and kicking the door but I was determined not to yield to his cries. I was his wife—beaten, bruised and bereft by years of mistreatment from a man who had no aspiration in life.

Earlier that day, Jim had had a quarrel with our neighbor, Ben, who had accused him of littering on his lawn. In this acrimonious dispute both of them made threatening remarks and almost got into a fistfight. Their wild behavior was like that of two angry dogs wanting to tear each other apart. I had to struggle to keep them separated. After this quarrel, Jim stormed off to get drunk again.

Over the years, Jim's unruly behavior had greatly affected my reputation. Since I lived with him and tolerated his profanity, people who disliked him had begun to think less of me. Our friends and neighbors who had once welcomed me and treated me with respect now shunned me. Their coldness froze my self-respect, and each day became more distressful. I felt they were being unfair to me for I had done no wrong and, in fact, had always made a special effort to follow ethical precepts. I could not understand why they should punish me for Jim's actions. Being an active member in the community church, I felt totally humiliated by all that was happening.

Knowing that Jim was short-tempered, I decided not to argue with him. I kept the doors locked and remained silent in the house. For a moment, he stopped banging and I felt relieved, thinking he had left. Just as I switched the lights off in my room and was about to lie down in bed, I heard a fusillade of gunshots. My heart began racing and for a moment I thought that I was going to have a heart attack. I stood still for a few minutes before rushing to the front door. I gasped in shock at the sight of Jim lying on the front lawn with Ben our neighbor standing over him with a gun in his hand.

Jim had been shot four times in the chest. As soon as Ben saw me coming, he rushed back into his house with his finger still on the trigger of the gun. For a moment I felt vindictive and began to follow him, but seconds later my religious sentiments took hold and I decided not seek revenge. I was furious with him for taking the law into his own hands, thinking that what he had done to Jim was premeditated. I turned and hurried back to help Jim, but was stunned by what I saw. Even as he lay bleeding to death, he clung to his bottle of alcohol. I shook my head in disbelief when I saw him trying to put his mouth around the bottle.

I stared at my inebriated and helpless husband and watched the blood gushing out of his body. In an intense outburst of anger I grabbed the bottle from his hand and flung it high into the air. My bitterness for the years of torture almost made me turn away, but my strong moral convictions stopped me from abandoning him. I was, after all, his wife and therefore bound by duty to treat him with kindness and respect. In his moment of misfortune I could not possibly leave him to suffer.

Jim was bleeding profusely from the upper part of his chest. I realized that I had to act quickly. As I looked around wildly for help I saw a man standing some distance away from me with his arms folded and gazing at the sky, completely oblivious to the incident. His nonchalance agitated me. In a commanding voice I yelled at him to come quickly and assist me to move Jim. Being a nurse, I knew that if I could get him back into the house I could ease the bleeding by tending to his wound. I knew it would take quite some time for the police and paramedics to arrive since we lived in a rural area.

It was dark outside and I could not get a clear view of the stranger, who seemed to be wandering aimlessly. Since he was not responding to my call, I took a bold step and approached him with ferocity. I grabbed him by the hand, and forcefully pulled him over to the place where Jim was lying. In a strong voice I told him to help me lift Jim into the house. Surprisingly, he did not utter a single word but did exactly as he was told.

It was tough for both of us to get Jim into the house. With my hands practically covered in blood from holding him, I found it fatiguing to get a solid enough grip on his body to lift him. Apart from struggling to hold him up, I had to stop frequently to adjust my loose-fitting night-dress from revealing my breasts to the stranger. To get this man to concentrate on what he was doing was difficult, for he seemed confused by the surroundings and all that was happening. I had to constantly yell and pull him by the hand. For a moment I thought he was drunk, because he could not walk properly and his actions were awkward. I was so anxious to get Jim into the house that I did not stop for a moment to ask him any questions about himself.

Inside the house, the stranger looked totally exhausted, for he sat on the floor breathing heavily. With the lights of the house now on I could see his face more clearly. He was a bearded man in his mid-forties whose face was like that of a corpse. His pale lips were dry, cracked and practically covered with scab. The hairs from his nostrils were long and seemed as though they had never been trimmed. His hands looked soft like those of a woman and his fingernails were long and curved. From the tips of his nails I could see droplets of blood trickling along his fingers. He must have hurt them from trying to move Jim. Since his injury was a minor one I ignored his bleeding.

While tending to Jim I frequently glanced at the stranger who sat barefooted with his legs wide apart. From his primitive behavior and his appearance, he seemed more suited to a society that had existed centuries ago. It suddenly came to me that I had seen him before. He belonged to the science laboratory of the local hospital where medical scientists had recently succeeded in bringing him back to life. Momentarily stunned by recognizing this man, I could not decide immediately whether to inform the police.

I was not afraid of him because he looked harmless and piteous. In the short time since we met I sensed a degree of innocence in his behavior and felt he could easily be misled. Thinking about the numerous medical tests and experiments that scientists would be performing on him, I developed a strong feeling of compassion for this man.

It was only a week ago that I had learned that doctors had revived this man and were treating him with medication and a liquid diet of nourishing foods. At the hospital everyone referred to him as the Cryonic Man, for he had died over one hundred years ago. His frozen body was discovered in one of the coldest regions on earth and was brought to the local hospital where medical scientists worked fastidiously to bring him back to life. At this hospital, which was close to my home, I worked as a nurse in a separate department where I was assigned to monitor and take care of patients who were on life support machines. It seemed clear to me that this man was probably left unattended at night and had walked out of the hospital.

As a religious person, I felt that what these doctors were doing was unethical and I was totally against it. Before calling the police to report the shooting of my husband, I hurriedly grabbed the stranger by the hand, took him down into the basement and locked the door. I hurried back up the stairs but stopped abruptly when I heard an earsplitting scream from the stranger. Seconds later, my dog Leo began to bark frantically. Immediately, I placed my hands over my face and shook my head in disbelief at what I had done. I had made a terrible mistake by locking him inside the basement with my dog. Rushing back down I fumbled with the lock and nervously opened the door. Lying half-naked on the floor was the stranger being savagely attacked by the dog. Hurriedly, I grabbed Leo by the collar and pulled him off, leaving the stranger totally stunned. Leo continued to snarl at the man, but I finally managed to calm him down, drag him out of the house and put him into his kennel.

I rushed back to the frightened man to see the extent of his injuries. Luckily, they were not serious, he was only bitten on the hands and legs. I had to return upstairs to help Jim, so I quickly shut the basement door and locked up the stranger once more. I wanted to conceal his where-abouts from the scientists who might treat him like a guinea pig for their own selfish aims.

By the time I got back to Jim, he was lying on the floor, face down, dead. I turned him over on his back and straightened his hands and feet. With so much going through my mind I closed my eyes to think clearly. In a calmer frame of mind I decided to inform the police.

In this residential neighborhood where the majority of houses are built far apart, it wasn't common for people to hear gunshots or see patrol cars. But with so much police activity following the shooting, people began to gather in front of my home to find out what had happened. When several police officers began asking for eyewitnesses, they all came to know that Jim had been killed.

That night, Ben was arrested and taken away for questioning. As soon as the detectives had left I wept and blamed myself for Jim's death, for had I let him into the house, this tragedy might not have occurred. I was so upset that I totally forgot about the man whom I had locked up in the basement.

The next couple of days were hectic, with the police and the funeral arrangements. I got a priest to perform his final rites for I strongly believed in prayer in times of grief. While Jim lay in his coffin waiting to be cremated I performed a short ritual by lighting a candle and holding it while I circumambulated his body three times. Although he had desecrated his body while he lived, what I performed symbolized the dignity and respect that is owed to the human body, even if it were done as a final rite.

At the funeral I saw my elder sister June, who hadn't spoken to me in over three and a half years. I was taken by surprise when she came up to me to offer her condolences. She and I were not on friendly terms due to a family dispute we had over Jim's behavior. June never wanted me to marry Jim because she claimed he had a split personality and could be very violent, especially under the influence of alcohol.

For the greater part of the funeral service June sat among fellow churchgoers who had also come to pay their final respects to the deceased. Together they sang hymns and uttered prayers for Jim, in hope that he would be forgiven for all his wrong doings. As the ceremony was slowly coming to an end, my sister June gave me a shock when she walked up to the pulpit to give a short eulogy. Her giving this homily incensed me by its hypocrisy. I could not see how she had the gall to talk about how greatly Jim would be missed when she had shunned us so openly during his life.

When all was said and done she came over to me and politely requested that we both put aside our differences and renew our sisterly relationship once more. As her sister I felt that it was my duty to maintain a harmonious relation with her. However, even if we did, I must admit that my feelings for her as a sister were never to be the same again. I felt that June and her friends had been unfair to me by judging me, not on the merit of my own actions, but as an addition to Jim whom they had despised.

*   *   *

The enmity between Jim and my sister started seven weeks before I got married. Jim claimed that June called him a drunken bastard; June, on the other hand, denied this and claimed that Jim was intoxicated one night and shouted obscene language at her. I was not present so it was difficult to say who was right or who was wrong.

From the first day I got married to Jim, my sister June developed a terrible attitude towards me. Being disappointed with my marriage, she became jealous of whatever little material or financial success Jim and I acquired in matrimony. In short, she did not want to see me prosper in life while married to the man she hated.

June was the type of person who held steadfast to her opinion and who liked to win in every conversation. She had a habit of arguing over trivial things until others conceded to her views. When displeased, June could become insidious: on the surface she would smile gently, but deep in her heart she harbored feelings of resentment. However, in spite of what she had to say about Jim, nothing at that time could have deterred me from marrying him, because I was young and very much in love with him.

Knowing that June was pompous and choosy, even in finding a suitable husband for herself, I paid little attention to what she advised. Being praised and admired for her beauty, June grew to be proud and egocentric. Her vanity made her believe that she was too good for ordinary men, and as a result she delayed getting married to anyone.

At age twenty she lived in a world of fantasy. She spent hours daily tending to her hair, putting on make-up and admiring herself in front of the mirror. She loved to attract people's attention with her fashionable clothing, and enjoyed their compliments. It was her desire to find and marry a perfect gentleman whom she conceived to be rich, righteous, and trustworthy. This, however, proved not to be the case for she remained unmarried and that suitable one never came along.

June and I attended the same church every Sunday, so it was distressing to see my own sister and not be able to communicate with her. Over the years I had made several attempts to renew our sisterly ties, but on all occasions June would either ignore me or walk away from me.

Unlike my sister, I paid little attention to one's character and this in the end made me regret marrying Jim. Being young and in love with Jim I turned a blind eye to his personality, even though I knew he could become a little rowdy under the influence of alcohol.

Jim's addiction to alcohol was not the result of being unemployed or any other unfavorable circumstances. It began when he started drinking at social gatherings and among friends who were party-goers. As his drinking increased, he slowly became hooked on alcohol and could no longer control his addiction. As an alcoholic, he did not feel that he had a drinking problem. What was joy to him was a major distress for me. Jim claimed that alcohol gave him a delightful feeling which, in his view, was far greater than the joy I found in living a religious life.

Jim hated my involvement with the church and accused me of worshipping God out of fear and out of a desire to be rewarded for my good deeds. He always insisted that I study the role of human beings on Earth and how they interact with the environment. He believed that if I did this, my concept of God would change as I would become more inclined to think rationally. With both of us having opposing beliefs in almost everything, we weren't compatible as a married couple.

From the earliest stage of my marriage to Jim, June had always encouraged me to divorce him. She could not accept him as part of our family. Because I was reluctant to separate from him she decided not to speak to either of us. Though I disliked some of June's habits and the things she said about Jim, I did not hold a grudge against her. Now that I am older I can understand that, as my elder sister, she was only trying to protect me from a marriage which she honestly felt would bring me sorrow. I must admit that in the end she was right in advising me not to marry Jim, for whatever she said about him proved later to be true.

Jim's death was sudden and shocking and left me distraught. I never thought that we would become separated by death. Divorce perhaps, given his dissolute ways, but never death. All my hate, anger and resentment melted away. All I felt was anguish, and my only comfort came from my faith in God.

CHAPTER 2

On the third day after Jim's death, it suddenly dawned upon me that the Cryonic Man was still locked up in the basement, but when I returned to the house he was nowhere in sight. Immediately, I went into a panic and began a desperate search for him. I noticed that some of the fruits that were in a basket on top of my freezer were eaten and the skins were left scattered in front of the washroom door. From the toilet I heard odd, slurping noises. I cautiously approached the door and slowly turned the knob, and there before me was the stranger down on his knees drinking water from the toilet bowl! His beard and mustache were completely soaked. My sudden appearance made him jump with a convulsive movement. He then looked at me blankly with his eyes and mouth open wide in fear. To calm him down I patted him affectionately on the shoulder and told him not to worry. I realized that, since he was born generations ago, it was impossible for him to know about modern washrooms, the telephone and electricity.

In days to follow I began to teach him things. Having been inactive for such a long time he could not walk straight and at times staggered like a drunken man. I gave him the name Josh, and bit by bit I began to teach him to speak more clearly. The most difficult thing for him to learn was how to use the modern appliances inside the house.

Josh became very attached to me and treated me as though I were his parent. He was humble, warm and affectionate and seemed pleased and contented with what was offered to him. His innocence made me afraid that he could easily be deceived or misled by people with bad intentions. At times, his behavior was like that of a child as he frequently followed me around the house, being inquisitive about everything I did. He found my modern radio amusing and treated it like a toy. A curious Josh often fiddled with the control knobs to vary the volume and to hear the different voices of radio broadcasters. I never felt there was any danger in what he was doing until a serious incident made me realize that I had to keep a close eye on almost everything that he did. While tending to my laundry one evening, I heard a sudden cry from Josh and then a loud bang on the adjacent wall from me. Rushing into the living room, I saw Josh on the floor trembling with fright. I discovered that he had found a nail somewhere in the house, and while pushing it into a small opening of the radio, he suffered a minor electric shock. Minutes later, he regained his composure and I felt relieved that nothing serious had happened.

In getting to know Josh, I realized that both of us were compatible in many ways in that we communicated well with each other and enjoyed similar things. However, my relationship with him was not the same as in matrimony for we did not share the same bed nor had any desire to unite in sex.

Before leaving for work the following day, I locked him inside the house and warned him not to go outside. I felt guilty treating him like a prisoner, but I was only trying to protect him from being kept in confinement by doctors who were eagerly waiting to do a series of medical tests on him. At work I discovered that there was a massive hunt for Josh by the police, and his face was on the front page of every newspaper. His back-to-life adventure had sparked nation-wide attention, as people eagerly wanted to learn about his after-death experiences.

Returning from work later that day, I hurriedly entered the house and began calling his name. Not getting any answer I searched every room in the house. I could not find him anywhere. It was not until I entered the basement and discovered one of the windows open that I suspected he was out of the house. I raced out and began looking for him. As I pushed open the gate that led into the backyard, I was astonished to find Josh with his pants down, defecating on my lawn. Though I felt terribly embarrassed by what he was doing, I realized there was no time for me to be bashful or coy. Immediately, I hurried him to put his pants back on and began pulling him by the hand towards the house.

It was not an easy task to get him quickly into the house because his loose-fitting pants kept falling off. While I pulled him, Leo in the kennel began barking furiously. Without warning, the enraged canine forced its way out of the kennel and came charging towards Josh.

Josh let go of his pants and started running around the yard, while I desperately struggled to keep the dog at bay. This was probably the most embarrassing thing that had ever happened to me, since I was running after a furious dog that was chasing a man with no pants or underwear on.

After a hectic struggle I managed to gain control of Leo, and this time I made sure that he was locked securely in the pen. Then I hurriedly pulled Josh by the hand back into the house. I realized that I had completely forgotten to show him how to use the indoor toilet. It now occurred to me that, in the era in which Josh once lived, it might have been customary to use the outdoors as a toilet.

My only fear at this point was whether my neighbors had seen him in the act. Inside the house, I hurried Josh to take a shower. Thinking that the police might soon come to my home looking for him, I quickly decided to change his appearance. After his shower, I trimmed his hair, cut his nails and shaved his beard off. I gave him a set of brand-new clothing and forced him to wear my sunglasses. He looked very uncomfortable wearing them, but now I was confident that no one could tell who he was.

Minutes later, I heard a loud knocking on my front door. Sensing that it was the police, I hurriedly grab my handbag and pretended that Josh and I were about to leave the house. During the time that he lived at my house I had never mentioned to him that he was wanted by the police. I tried not to create any fear in his mind of people wanting to harm him. But now, since the police might ask him if he had seen a stranger in the neighborhood, I told him he must say "no" if questioned.

Opening the front door I saw two tall, heavily built policemen, one of whom politely asked if we had seen a strange man in our neighborhood. Josh spontaneously replied "no!" To prevent him from answering any further questions, I quickly told the officer that I was employed at the local hospital and aware of the missing person. The officers quietly left and went over to my neighbor's house. Knowing that the police had seen us preparing to leave the house, I had no choice but to leave immediately with Josh.

It was the first time for Josh to be driven in a car and I was nervous about what might happen. The moment we got out of the house I told him quietly to follow me towards the car. I carefully led him to the passenger side of the vehicle and quickly opened the door. I knew it would be difficult to convince him to get inside the car, so I cautiously looked around and then quickly pushed him into the vehicle and shut the door. I then got quietly into the car and slowly drove away, again trying to show no signs of suspicion. I drove for half an hour in the countryside, hoping that by this time the police would have left my neighborhood.

Throughout our short journey, Josh remained obedient and did exactly as I had told him, to remain silent. He sat upright and tense in the car, perhaps afraid that it might crash at any moment. Now and again, he moved his head to look in wonder at the long and winding roads on which luxurious cars frequently passed. This was probably the most exciting experience of his life, for he looked totally spellbound by the wonders of modern developments.

As we turned the final corner on our way home, I saw the same police officers in a parked car in front of my house. Josh sat next to me quiet and undaunted. He had absolutely no idea that he was wanted by the police. As I stepped out of the car, I was approached by both officers who began asking me a series of questions. I was told that one of my neighbors had seen a strange man in my backyard and that I was seen with him. To protect Josh, I denied seeing or meeting anyone, and to remove any suspicion, I suggested that they search my home.

The officers made a complete search of the house and could not find anyone. As they were leaving, one of the officers went over to the passenger side of the vehicle to question Josh. Josh did exactly as I had told him, by saying no to all questions. His firm and negative replies made the officer suspicious, thinking he was withholding information.

One of the officers asked Josh to get out of the vehicle but once again he replied no. The policeman opened the door, grabbed him by the arm and started pulling him out of the car. Being manhandled, Josh began to fight back, and in this confrontation the officer pulled out his gun and shot Josh in the abdomen. He slumped over with his head leaning against the dashboard of the car. Quickly, the officer began to pass his hands over his body to see if he was concealing a weapon, but found nothing. Opening the door on the driver side of the car, the other officer quickly pushed him back to lean against the seat. He then pulled out his gun and pointed it straight at Josh's chest. I could not comprehend why this officer was aiming for Josh's heart in spite of him being unarmed and wounded. Watching the serious intent on the faces of these two policemen, it seemed to me that they were only trained to aim for the heart and not at the feet of a wounded man. Thinking that the officer was going to shoot Josh a second time, I yelled at him to put away his gun. He slowly withdrew his weapon.

Josh was then taken out of my car and put into the police vehicle where he was quickly transported to the local hospital. I was deeply saddened by the outcome of this misunderstanding, for Josh was never involved in any crime, but he ended up being treated like a criminal.

CHAPTER 3

The science department of the hospital was a place of bustling activity. Here, the police were conducting an investigation about the Cryonic Man who had left the hospital. Although Josh was a patient of this hospital no one suspected him of being the missing person. With his hair cut and his face cleanly shaven it was difficult for anyone to identify him.

After weeks in hospital, the wound in his abdomen became a major concern to many doctors because the healing process was slow and painful for him. Besides his infirmities, he had a cadaverous look and had to remain under the watchful eyes of doctors.

One day when I came to visit him in the hospital, I was taken by surprise to see him surrounded by nurses and doctors. Immediately, I felt that something had gone wrong. As I eased my way through to look at him I realized that I had lost the struggle to conceal his identity. Josh had been in hospital over six weeks and by this time the hairs on his face had grown back to their original length. He looked exactly the way I had seen him when we first met. The scientists identified him as the man they were in search of, and were delighted to find him. Fearing that he might try to escape again, they handcuffed his hands to the bed and began making plans to move him to a new department in the hospital.

I decided to leave the hospital. On my way out, I noticed that hundreds of people were gathering in front of the building. News spread quickly about the Cryonic Man being discovered in hospital. As the crowd grew larger, a number of police were called in to dislodge trespassers. This, however, did not deter photographers, the media and the public from gathering in front of the hospital.

I learned later that it was impossible to dissuade people from wanting to see the Cryonic Man, so the hospital officials decided to let the public have a short look at him. Their secret plan was to move him out of the hospital for a short while and then bring him back later. They were hoping to trick the large crowds into believing that he would no longer be kept at this location and they would have to search elsewhere.

To make a good presentation of the Cryonic Man, they removed his handcuffs, put him in a wheelchair and slowly pushed him out of the building. Seeing this large gathering of people for the first time, Josh looked as if he had awakened from a horrifying dream. As he was pushed through a crowd of photographers and hundreds of people staring at him, he moved his head from side to side as if he had no idea where he was. With people pushing in every direction to get a glimpse of him, he became terrified and attempted to get out of his chair. However, the paramedics quickly forced him back into his seat and pushed him through the crowd into their vehicle.

After everyone had left, Josh was secretly brought back to the hospital later that night, where doctors continued to monitor his health. He could not be taken to any other location to be treated since this hospital was the most advanced in terms of medical facilities and technology.

On my way home I began to think of ways to free Josh who was now undergoing even more mental suffering. I realized that, with him being kept under the watchful eyes of the hospital staff, it was impossible for me to attempt freeing him. The only thing I could do was to give him support in his time of misfortune.

In the past I had never disclosed to anyone that I was against the medical operations of these scientists. After Josh was discovered in hospital as the Cryonic Man, everyone became focused on learning about his after-death experiences and how he was brought back to life. They seemed to care less about his past or where he went into hiding when he was first discovered missing. The police for unknown reasons stopped their investigation. My only guess was that the Cryonic Man was wanted not by police but by scientists.

Being a senior nurse at the hospital with many friends on the administrative level, I decided to ask to be transferred to the department where Josh was kept. And with a little help from my friends I soon became his assigned nurse.

Josh was the most talked-about person in the hospital, and was constantly visited by medical doctors from all regions of the country. When he saw me for the first time in hospital, dressed in my nurse's attire, he looked nervous thinking I was going to harm him. He was puzzled by the samples of blood that were extracted from his body and the sophisticated medical equipment that surrounded him. It was not until I told him that I had come here to help him that he became calmer.

It was difficult for me to communicate with Josh during the day because many influential people wanted to see him in person. But since visitors were not allowed at nights, I decided to change my work shift from day to night so that I could spend more time alone with him.

One night when it was least hectic at work, I quietly entered his room and saw him with his head down, looking totally dejected. As I sat down beside him, he slowly raised his head and said, "You must assist me to leave the Earth so that I can return to my true abode where there is everlasting peace." I was deeply touched by these words, but I realized that there was little I could do to help him. To make him feel better I promised that I would soon take him back to my home. But he seemed annoyed and insisted that he wanted to go back to his own home. I could not comprehend which home he was speaking of and thought that he was probably fabricating things. Nevertheless, Josh was not only tenacious about going home, but seemed confident about what he was saying. I wanted to question him on the subject but I realized that it was time for me to leave. I did not want to leave any signs of suspicion that I had been away too long tending to the patient.

The following night I came back to his room and began to encourage him to tell me about his after-death experiences and the place that he called home. Without any hesitation, Josh revealed to me this enthralling story.

*   *   *

He told me that, when he lived on Earth, he had died in a deep hole of ice. This sudden accident shattered his earthly dream, for when he was alive, he strongly desired to live a very long and healthy life. He claimed that prior to his death he used to drink daily a syrupy liquid made from certain proteins, fats and oils in the hope of preventing his body from aging or decaying after death. In the extremely cold region where he once lived with relatives and friends, he had worked as a gravedigger. He dug deep holes in the ice to bury the dead. He explained that one day while digging, the surrounding walls of ice caved in on him and he could not get out. With the heavy weight of ice on top of him he could no longer breathe, and he suddenly felt separated from his body. He felt as though he had awakened to start a new life without a physical body. He realized that he had died, and with this his thoughts abandoned his body and began seeking ways to come out of the hole.

In this dark place he could not see anything or find a way to escape. Then a narrow beam of light suddenly appeared through a crack in the ice. In this streak of light he was now able to see a part of his own body, which was covered in the heavy clothing he wore to protect himself from the harsh weather. This convinced him that his thoughts were now a separate form of existence from his body. Suddenly, it dawned upon him to follow the light and in doing so he felt guided by it. Seconds later, he felt relieved for he was out of the hole and quickly rising into the air. On his way up he fell into a dreamlike state, and he started to encounter a mixture of both good and bad experiences.

Josh related that shortly before the ice caved in on him, something mysterious occurred. While he was digging the ice, a stray dog suddenly appeared and stood over the hole, looking down at him. The animal raised its head towards the sky and started to howl in a mournful way. This sudden cry from the dog greatly annoyed him, so to stop the strange sound, he picked up a hardened piece of ice and threw it at the animal. Struck under the neck, the dog quickly turned and ran away.

Minutes later, a stray cat with piercing eyes appeared and began to walk cautiously around the hole. Now and again, the cat stopped to stare down at him inquisitively. Suddenly, the cat jumped into the hole and began to rub its body against his feet as though it wanted to be comforted. Irritated by what the cat was doing, he shrugged it off with his feet. This did not deter the cat from coming back and doing the same thing once more. He grew frustrated by being interrupted, and in a fury he picked up the cat and flung it into the air, out of the hole. Shortly afterward, dark, ominous clouds slowly drifted in the sky and momentarily covered the light of the sun.

These weird occurrences made him think about an irrational belief his mother had. As a young boy he had learned from her that certain birds, cats and dogs could sense when a human being was going to die. His mother believed that if a certain raven-like bird or cat sensed that someone was likely to die, the creature might lurk around the home of their relative or friend. His mother also associated the mournful howling of a dog with death because the animal senses that someone is gravely ill and in danger of losing his or her life. She believed that, even though the presence of these creatures might be considered a bad omen, one should not treat them inhumanely because of their sudden appearance in times of distress. She felt that these creatures experience similar feelings to those of human beings; they too experience ill luck and are afraid of death. In a sorrowful frame of mind they may come to

a home where there is grief to share in one's sorrows. It was while thinking about this superstitious belief of his mother that the surrounding
walls of ice suddenly caved in and killed him.

*   *   *

From the time he died, this journey in his sleep seemed to last several
decades, and it appeared to him that this mixture of good and bad experiences was gradually healing his thoughts. The duration of this journey
depended on the merit of his actions on Earth. The bad experiences he
encountered were a form of suffering that he had to endure because of
the wrongful things he had done on Earth, such as robbing the dead of
their clothing and jewelry.

In the good experiences he met with people from all walks of life,
sharing with them moments of grief. And from these experiences he
began to learn the importance of good conduct. Gradually, he started to
become righteous in his thinking, and soon he was able to understand
how everything worked in harmony with acts of virtue.

Of all the experiences he encountered, one remained the most memorable. He dreamed that he was miraculously transported to an island
which was surrounded by a turbulent sea, where he met thousands of
people, including his wife, relatives and friends. On this island everyone
learned that in a couple of days the entire landmass would sink into the
sea. Certain that they were going to die, people began showering one
another with kindness and words of comfort. Fearing death, no one was
inclined to do anything sinful. The friendship among people was unbelievable. Being faced with similar circumstances they sought unity and
peace, and chose good over evil.

Believing that death was inescapable, people began making choices
of their own in preparation. While many abandoned all their riches,
others chose to dress in expensive clothing and deliberated over where

they would like to be and whom they would like to be with at the time of death.

In a small town on the island called Blenheim, a group of people began making beautifully decorated coffins and offered them to those who wished to lie in one prior to the great deluge. Some people who were afraid of dying at sea sought help from others who were offering a special drug to put them to death painlessly before the flood approached. Josh, being very much afraid of drowning, decided to take the drug which could kill him within a couple of hours. The moment he swallowed the drug, the thought of his wife and only son dawned on his mind. He instantly realized that he had made a hurried decision because he hadn't consulted his wife. With only a short time to live, he began a desperate search for his wife and child since he could not bear the thought of leaving them behind to die in the flood.

He uttered a silent prayer to God not to let him die during his search as he wanted to be reunited with his wife and child. Luckily, after an intense search, he found them, and they were delighted to see one another. Josh immediately told his wife about the deadly drug he had taken. She became greatly saddened and wept. An impatient Josh then began to plead with his wife to take the drug, but not to give it to their child for he could not bear the thought of taking the life of his own son. His wife, realizing that they would all die eventually, and that time was running out on Josh, decided to take the deadly drug. Josh then nervously indicated to his wife that he had one last desire to fulfill, and that was to tell the wife of his closest friend about the drug he had taken. He had known for many years that his friend's wife feared the open sea and did not want to die drowning. He wanted to find the married couple who was dear to his family, and encourage them to take the drug and join him and his family in dying together.

Before leaving, Josh advised his wife to take their son immediately to the town of Blenheim where coffins were made, to select a large coffin into which they would all fit, and to lie in it with their son until he returned. Josh begged his wife not to worry for he was confident that he could convince the couple to join them in dying together.

While Josh left in search of the married couple, his wife and son set out on their journey to the town of Blenheim. His wife developed a sorrowful feeling and began rethinking what Josh had told her to do. In a worrisome frame of mind, she decided to give her son the deadly drug, because she could not bear the thought of leaving him to die by himself in the flood.

While searching for the couple, Josh met many other friends, most of whom were deliberating whether to take the drug or not. Though he cared for them, he realized that he could not afford to spend too much time convincing them to take it since he had only a short time to live. Soon Josh began to feel the deadly effects of the drug. He realized that the more he exerted himself in this search, the weaker he would feel. Fearing that he might die suddenly, he began deliberating whether he should abandon his search for the couple and return to his wife. However, a strange thing happened: someone threw a small stone at him. It was his best friend who threw it to attract his attention. He became filled with joy when he saw the couple standing among a group of people and waving their hands at him. He hurried to greet them and told them about the deadly drug he had taken. His friend's wife fell into a melancholy mood for she realized that Josh was going to die sooner than she had expected. Josh pleaded with both of them to take the drug and follow him to the town of Blenheim where they would all die together. His friend, however, did not like the idea of taking the drug, and felt that Josh's decision was premature. On the other hand his friend's wife, who was afraid of dying in the flood, wanted to take the drug that Josh offered to her. She seemed anxious to follow Josh but sadly she could not leave without the consent of her husband. A disappointed Josh looked at the couple and tearfully said goodbye. Because of the short time he had to live, he realized that he could not spend any more time in convincing them to join him.

On his journey back to meet his wife and son, he started to feel dizzy and to walk unsteadily. Soon, he began to experience dry sensations in the mouth and became thirsty for water. With the thought of death racing through his mind, he realized that he could not afford to waste time in search of something to drink, and could only hope for a miraculous thing to happen. His perseverance seemed to be the one thing that kept him going against all odds. Suddenly, it became very windy and minutes later there was a torrential downpour of rain. He managed a faint smile, and looked towards the heaven to offer thanks to God. To quench his thirst, he slowly raised his head back and opened his mouth to drink the water which came from above. After drinking, he paused for a moment to look once again at the sky, but this time it looked dark and eerie. Believing that something dreadful was about to happen, Josh sank further into despair, fearing that he might not arrive in time to see his wife and child.

Continuing to walk in the pouring rain, Josh saw an elderly man stumble and fall to the ground because of the strong winds. As this helpless man struggled to get back on his feet, he debated whether to leave him on the ground or save his strength to make the journey to see his dying wife. His health was in a steady state of decline, but he uttered a silent prayer to God to grant him a little strength so that he could help this man. With the willpower to help, he ignored his infirmities and made a courageous effort to get the elderly man on his feet.

He passed his fingers through his wet hair to move it away from his eyes so that he could see where to walk and got a pleasant surprise, for he was able to see the place where the coffins were made. With a renewed feeling he was now confident that he would meet his family. However, it was not as easy as he had thought for, when he got there, he saw hundreds of coffins. He became nervous and confused since it was difficult to tell which of the coffins his wife and son were in. As he struggled to move from one coffin to the other in search of his family, he heard the crying voice of a young child. Looking anxiously around, he saw a young girl weeping. The girl began pleading with him to help her because she became separated from her parents in the storm. A confused Josh once again fell into a state of despair and began deliberating what to do. He stood in the pouring rain struggling to keep his weary eyes open. With hardly any strength to move, he was left with the tough choice to either answer the call of the helpless child or to join his wife and son, whom he desperately wanted to meet before their demise. Josh made the toughest of choices, even though he knew the odds were highly against him. By this time he had lost all strength to stand on his legs. With faith, courage and feelings of the heart, Josh crawled on his knees in an attempt to find the child's parents, and with this his dream ended abruptly.

At the end of this experience his unsettled thoughts became disciplined, and he was miraculously transported to a place of peace and bliss. This place was called Hadesheol, meaning the abode of the dead. He believed that those who performed good deeds would find the journey to Hadesheol to be short and pleasant, while those who performed ungodly acts would find it very long. Through years of bittersweet experiences on the journey to the abode of the dead, all those who have passed away on Earth will in the end become wholly righteous.

The planet Hadesheol was a hundred times larger than Earth. The minute he arrived, his ancestors and past friends came to greet him, and he was absolutely delighted. For a short while everyone looked exactly the same as when he had last seen them on Earth. However, their bodies then began to change into youthful ones and he was puzzled by this transformation; he too took on a youthful body. Here all races of people lived in peace and harmony. Their faces had a heavenly glow and their skin was smooth and wrinkle-free. After a while he realized that this transformation of the body was done every time someone new came to Hadesheol, so that relatives and friends could recognize one another.

While Josh lived on Earth, he had always thought that the abode of the dead was a place where the good and the bad would meet to be judged for their earthly actions. Instead, he found it to be a place where all dwelled in unity. The long journey to Hadesheol and the experiences he had encountered were a form of suffering he had to undergo for all the wicked things he had done on Earth. It was a slow process he had to undertake on the path of self-realization to become purely righteous.

Hadesheol was a place beyond the brightest star where darkness never existed. In this celestial abode thousands of mountains stood aloft and slowly drifted in the sky. The summits were flat and suitable for living, while the sides were all covered with emerald green vegetation. On top of these mountains hundreds of immortals visited colorful castles surrounded by gardens of immense beauty. From fountains water poured into enticing streams that were encircled by exotic flowers. Here, various colored pebbles sparkled like diamonds along magnificent walkways leading to decorative homes. The view from the summit was breathtaking, and everything seemed as if it were a part of God revealing Itself.

The land on the planet Hadesheol was rich in vegetation, with billions of trees bearing a wide variety of sweet fruits that carried all the essential nutrients to nourish their youthful bodies. The rich green grass was soft and felt good to walk on. There was food for all and freedom from desire and disease. Their minds had developed to the point where they had finally gained perfection. On this planet no one had money or owned anything of material value, hence there was nothing to quarrel or fight about. In the abode of the dead there was no sexual desire because people could not reproduce. Everyone dressed alike in long, soft, white robes. There were shady trees everywhere and, in this perfect environment, it was a wonderful place to relax among past relatives and friends.

        *   *   *

What Josh had to say about Hadesheol was startling and I began to debate with myself whether such a place truly existed. The more I reflected upon what he said, the more I had mixed views. Knowing that he had died over a hundred years ago and was able to recount what he had experienced, I came to believe that after the death of his body, his thoughts or true self had never really died. In coming back to life after a hundred years he had a lot to tell, proving that his thoughts were very active.

However, I felt that all the beautiful things he claimed to have seen in heaven were a figment of his imagination. Much of what he described, such as fairy-tale castles, mountains and breath-taking sights, were quite similar to what I had practically seen here on Earth. I believed that after he had died his thoughts, in seeking to find a place of peace and bliss, had begun to fabricate a heaven of his own liking. In my view, this extraordinary place he called Hadesheol was something he created with his thoughts to make him happy, and it was probably the perfect place for him to be after death. I honestly felt that he could not have resided in a true heaven, for I could not see the point in him being accepted in heaven and then suddenly sent back to Earth to suffer.

Josh began to plead with me to put him to death painlessly so that he could return to the abode of the dead. Being a religious person I felt this was totally unethical, so I could not promise him that. But to make him feel better I promised that as soon as he got over his illness I would provide him with a comfortable place to live.

A few weeks later, Josh returned to normal health and the doctors began making plans to transfer him to another location to conduct a series of medical tests. I realized that this would be an ongoing mental torture for Josh, since these scientists were determined to learn about his after-life experiences and how his body would react to various drugs. Using the latest technology they were now planning to preserve the bodies of some people who had died a natural death with hope that in the near future they might be able to bring them back to life. Being shot at, tied to a bed and constantly visited by doctors, Josh soon believed that he was different from others and something was certainly wrong with him. He came to hate them and to become very rebellious. In anger he often struggled to free himself from the bed that he was handcuffed to. He became very moody and unpredictable. With the exception of myself, he disliked everyone and thought of them as his enemies.

Doctors, realizing that Josh's mental condition was worsening, soon began making plans to perform a brain operation on him that would change the nature of his personality. This operation had been successfully performed on a number of prisoners who had had a violent temper. These scientists had discovered the cause of abnormal behavior, and they could thus correct this defect and give violent people a peaceful disposition. Fearing that they might want to perform the same operation on Josh, I began contemplating ways of getting him to escape from the hospital.

CHAPTER 4

It was about 9:45 p.m. when I began preparing to do my routine checks on the four patients who were under intensive care in the hospital. Apart from Josh, three of them were in a coma and kept alive by life support devices.

Before visiting these patients my assistant nurse and friend, Maria Delgrave, and I had a lengthy discussion on the subject of one's right to die. Maria strongly believed that these patients who were kept on life support should be taken off, since there was no medical hope for them to return to normal health. As a religious person, I could not support her views. I felt that as a nurse it was my duty to save and not to take away life.

Maria was a sensitive and garrulous woman who had a great deal of confidence in herself. She had a habit of assessing people's personality and forming her own opinion about them. She judged a person's character from the things they said, their actions and what others had to say about them. Sadly, she never paused for a moment to think about her own faults or to listen to what others had to say about her.

At work she was meticulous and very hard to please. Whenever we were assigned to a specific task I often found her to be uncompromising. In short, she always wanted to have things done her way. She was so temperamental at times that I had to be cautious and not say anything to offend her. I did not know what caused her mood to vary each day;

my only guess is that she never took the time to reflect upon her actions or to closely control her unstable mind.

In spite of these weaknesses, I tried to maintain good relations with her since I felt that she was not entirely a bad person. Though many ignored her during conversations, I often listened to her attentively since most of what she had to say usually came to pass. I felt that her intentions were good when sharing her knowledge and experiences with others, never wanting others to experience hurt or regret.

Apart from being a qualified nurse, Maria was quite versed on the subjects of human anatomy and genetics. She was supportive of the work of many doctors who had successfully performed medical surgery on the brain, to change the behavior of people who were violent and considered a threat to society.

Maria believed that her hereditary characteristics helped to shape the way she thought, and the rate at which she learned things. She once told me that from a tender age she had surpassed many who were much older than she, with her ability to learn things. I did not fully support her idea, for I was puzzled by the fact that both of her parents had no formal education or specialized skills and yet Maria and her sisters turned out to be highly intelligent.

Hearing what Josh had said about his after-life experiences led me to believe that life for the majority of people is a cycle of birth and rebirth. It appeared that after death one's true self sets out on a dream-like journey in search of a place of peace and bliss. Here, it fabricates a heaven of its own making where it might dwell forever. If one's true self is not healed from these after-life experiences, it may take on another human body to continue in another cycle. What is learnt may vary with each person, for in a dream-like state each individual fabricates different things. With every cycle of birth one's true self picks up new experiences, thus keeping itself on a path of progressive development.

In analyzing Maria's beliefs and mine, I came to believe that the desire for knowledge from a tender age is influenced by one's past experiences in a previous life as well as the hereditary characteristics of one's parents.

Maria did not believe in a personal God who could help her in times of trouble. Instead, she viewed God as the Universe in its entirety and thought of It as an Infinite One that performs perpetual action. She believed that the knowledge achieved in medical research and used to help others is a part of this action. In her view, the Lord works in mysterious ways through the various forms of action to sustain all that emanates from Itself.

Maria's religious beliefs were very different from mine. I personally felt that most of what she believed in might be deeply rooted in mysticism. However, I must admit that though she was not overly religious, she was worthy of admiration for she was very compassionate to the sick and the elderly.

Because of my religious beliefs I felt it was unethical for surgeons to correct brain disorders of people who were incarcerated because of violent crimes. It was on this subject of science and religion that Maria and I got into an argument that night. Neither of us yielded to the other's beliefs; we became angry with each other and went our separate ways.

Returning to my workstation, I gathered my files and then left to do my routine checks on Josh and the other patients. Entering his room I discovered that Josh was practically falling asleep, so I decided not to disturb him.

Looking at him with his hands tied to the bed, I felt that it was an inhumane way to treat the sick. However, I had to obey the rules of the administration who feared that he might try to escape. I covered him with a blanket up to the waist and quietly left to continue my routine checks on the other patients, who shared a large room adjacent to Josh's.

Approximately fifteen minutes later I returned to Josh's room because I had forgotten to initial the report form to indicate the last time I had visited him. Now he appeared sound asleep. I turned down his light and was about to leave the room when I noticed that the blanket was pushed up to his chest. For some reason I doubted myself and thought I must have moved the blanket up when I visited him earlier. Since his hands were tied to the bed, I felt there was no reason for me to be suspicious about anything. With everything seemingly right, I quietly left his room and headed towards the washroom.

Later that night I decided to visit Maria to apologize for the quarrel we had had earlier. But I was surprised that Maria was not at her desk. I became a little concerned, as it was common practice for us to notify each other when leaving our work area. I decided to return to my workstation and continue with the routine visits to my patients. Entering Josh's room, I discovered that he was still asleep, so I quietly left to visit the other patients. I was horrified to see that the life support devices of these three patients were removed and practically ripped apart.

In panic I ran down the corridor yelling for Maria, who came running towards me upon hearing my call. She looked very scared, sensing something terrible must have happened, and unwittingly bumped into a loaded cart of medical supplies, bringing them crashing to the floor. I felt sorry when I saw her stumbling to her knees and then crawling a few feet on the floor before she could get up to ask what had gone wrong. Nervously I told Maria what had happened and requested that she get a doctor immediately. She limped away, hurrying to get help, and within minutes, two doctors arrived. Checking for a heartbeat, they discovered that these three patients were dead. In panic they rushed over to Josh's room, thinking that he too might require medical help; however, they found him lying in bed with his hands still handcuffed. At this point Josh was completely ruled out as a suspect in these murders.

Later, a number of police officers arrived at the hospital and began asking Maria and me questions about what had happened. Based on the information we gave, we both became suspected of murder. Within days both of us were summoned to appear in court to stand trial for these killings. I had not committed these murders, but knowing that Maria was in favor of euthanasia, I suspected her.

The court trial in this case was short, for Maria surprisingly pleaded guilty to the killings. I felt very much relieved by her answer since I was not prepared to stand a lengthy trial. She was sentenced to thirty-five years of incarceration with no conditional release. In this trial, I felt that justice was properly served for she had had no right to take the law into her own hands.

The night after the trial I found it difficult to sleep, as my mind was actively rehearsing the events of the day. It was about 11:30 p.m. that night when I heard a repetitive knock on my front door. As I slowly drew the curtains to see who it was, I was taken aback by the sight of Josh. I quickly unlocked the door to let him in. Seeing him standing in front of me was unbelievable, as I could not fathom how he had gotten out of the hospital. Guessing that someone must have brought him to my house, I quickly stepped out onto the front porch to see, but surprisingly there was no one in sight.

From the moment Josh entered the house he looked annoyed and twitchy, constantly scratching his legs and buttocks. I discovered that he was practically covered with ants, crawling all over his clothing. As I began to examine him more carefully I also observed that his hands and feet were soiled with mud. Astonished by what I saw, I questioned him about what had happened. Josh explained that he had escaped through the rear door of the hospital, and then made his way into an open field of tall grass and trees. Through this dark, muddy field he desperately searched for a path that led to my home. I realized that he was telling the truth, since I was quite familiar with this huge land site between my house and the rear of the hospital. Strangely, he could not explain how he came in contact with the tiny ants. I came to the conclusion that in the dark, he had accidentally stepped into a formicary during his escape.

I advised him to remove his clothing immediately to get rid of the ants. However, while doing this, a number of ants crawled up his nostrils which made him wildly excited. In confusion he started to jump up and down and push his forefinger up his nose, and he began screaming as though someone were attacking him. It was very unusual to see a grown man behave like this. Fearing that my neighbors might hear him screaming, I quickly pounced on him and held him firmly to the ground. I yelled at him to blow through his nostrils, and luckily as soon as he did this he got some relief. Using a wet cloth I quickly removed the remaining ants from other parts of his body.

In analyzing Josh's behavior over the last few months, I felt convinced that he was developing a character disorder from the series of unfortunate things that were happening to him. It was gradually becoming more difficult for me to predict how he would react when faced with situations in which he felt threatened.

Later that night, Josh looked fully relieved of what was bothering him. Now that he was much more composed, I asked him how he had escaped from the hospital. I learned that a few days before those patients had their life support equipment removed, Maria had visited him in his room and told him of her plan to set him free. He said she was kind to him for she showed him how to open the handcuffs and gave him the key to keep. She then made a promise to return one day to help him escape from the hospital. He said that he waited patiently for Maria to return but she never came back to help him.

While Josh was explaining, I realized that on the night of the killings, he was only pretending to be asleep. This would explain why the blanket seemed out of place—he had moved it himself with his freed hands. Josh went on to say that, after I had left the room the second time, he came out of his room and saw no one. Peeking into the nearby room, he saw the three other patients who looked as though they were being punished like him. He claimed that at this point he felt sorry for them and decided to set them free, so he removed all the devices that were attached to their hands and mouth. I realized that he did not understand the need for those life support devices. Afterward he went back to his room and again handcuffed himself to the bed.

This shocking revelation by Josh made me angry with Maria, for I strongly believed she had toyed with his emotions and made it possible for him to commit these murders without being clear about the ramifications of his actions. I now realized that Josh might one day be held responsible for these killings, and since Maria was in prison, at some point in time she might reveal the truth that Josh was the true killer. I believed she was only withholding this information because of her involvement in these murders. In the event of an appeal or second trial, the missing key to Josh's handcuffs might be a crucial piece of evidence in determining who had truly committed these murders. Fearing that Josh might be imprisoned if he were later found guilty, I decided to keep him in hiding until I could think of the most appropriate thing to do.

At noon the following day I received a letter from the justice department informing me that the court trial which involved my husband's death would commence in another week. When I told Josh about this he seemed totally unconcerned. I realized that it was difficult for him to comprehend what was involved in a murder trial as it was something new to him.

Before leaving for work the next day, I prepared a tasty meal for two. Josh appeared much more relaxed than the day before, and I was delighted to see him in such a pleasant mood. At the dinner table we sat opposite each other with a lighted candle in the center. Though the table was neatly covered with a red tablecloth and laid with fancy cutlery and empty wineglasses, the atmosphere could not be described as romantic. Josh paid little attention to me and seemed to enjoy only one thing, the food he ate. I could safely describe him as having no lustful desire since he appeared unfeeling and naive about love. After this quiet and enjoyable dinner it was time for me to leave, but first I told him to lock the door and to remain inside the house.

Returning from work early the next morning, I was taken by surprise to see a number of policemen and an ambulance in front of my neighbor's house. Though it was raining heavily, it did not deter me from inquiring what had happened for I felt something must have gone wrong. Seconds later, two paramedics carried a body into their vehicle. I wondered if Ben's mother had passed away, because I knew she had been sickly for some time. However, it had to be something of a more serious nature because of the numerous police vehicles present. As I eased my way through the parked vehicles to take a closer look, I was told by police not to go any further because someone had been killed. My neighbor Ben had been brutally murdered. Minutes later, two policemen approached me and began asking questions. For some reason they considered me a suspect in this murder because Ben had murdered my husband and his trial was due to commence in a week. I had only seen Ben once after Jim's death for he kept indoors while out on bail.

Any suspicion that the police might have had about my involvement in Ben's death quickly ended when I told them that I was now returning from work and had not been at home on the night of the murder. They checked with the administration of the hospital to verify my story and let me go.

As I was about to leave the scene and walk home, Ben's mother suddenly approached me and began accusing me of murdering her son. I had never seen her so loquacious and full of hate in all the years that I had known her. This feeble woman in her mid-eighties was totally shaken by the loss of her only son. From the grim expression on her face I could tell she was furious with me. With us living next to each other, she probably felt I had taken revenge by killing her son. To appease the situation I kept quiet and avoided talking back to her, realizing that she was deeply hurt by the loss of her son, and in this moment of grief, she could not contain her emotions. But Ben's mother grew more enraged and began pointing her umbrella in my face in a threatening manner. As she nervously moved closer to argue with me, her voice cracked with emotions and her frail body trembled. I realized that my presence was making her incensed, so I decided to leave.

As I stood on the front porch of my house and looked towards Ben's home, I began to reflect on some of his habits and the things that made him such an unusual character. Ben was a short, bald, fussy man in his mid-forties. He lived alone with his aging mother who had been constantly in and out of the hospital. Ben spent a great deal of time tending to his plants and the surroundings of his house. He was weird. For instance, once a week he mowed his lawn with only his shirt and underwear on and constantly muttered to himself. Ben often mistreated his playful dog for not doing as it was told. I can never forget the day when he whipped his dog for barking unnecessarily and then poured buckets of water on the animal to quiet him.

To this day I still remember one particular incident when Ben had asked a number of people, including myself, to join him in a public demonstration to protest government cut-backs to hospitals. Because his mother was sickly and had to be rushed often to the emergency department of the hospital, he grew frustrated with the lengthy time she had to wait before being treated. Ben also wanted to see other changes in the way the government handled taxpayers' money. He was fed up with politicians for constantly promising tax cuts and then coming up with new ways of extracting money from people's earnings. During this demonstration Ben's voice was loud and strong with occasional bursts of obscene language. He spoke passionately and wanted to let everyone know how he felt. After a while things got ugly when Ben and a few others began to hurl stones at police and public buildings. Because of the damage that was done, he was arrested, charged and fined over four thousand dollars for destroying public property. When I met Ben a few days later, he still seemed angry and wanted to know why had I not participated in the protest. I told him candidly that even though one has a right to demonstrate peacefully, they should abide by the law which forbids an ugly riot in which innocent people get hurt and public property gets destroyed.

In spite of Ben's strangeness, he had certain obliging qualities. Ben was not only the caretaker of our local church but he also volunteered to transport the elderly to church every Sunday morning. In church his voice was loud, strong and clear.

Ben could be described as an individual with a mixture of both good and bad qualities. While many will remember him for his outstanding service to the church, others will never forget that day when he hurled the most profane language at the driver of another vehicle for almost causing an accident. With so many contradictory qualities I wondered what part religion played in his life.

After the paramedics left with Ben's body, I entered my home, eager to find out what Josh had been doing while I was away. I could not find him upstairs, so I quickly ran down to the basement. I was taken by surprise to see Josh dressed in new clothes and watching television. I asked him if he had heard anything about Ben being murdered, and to my surprise he would not answer me. I became suspicious that he had done something wrong for he lowered his head to the side and refused to look at me. Concerned that he might be concealing something important, I repeatedly asked him whether he had gone out of the house during the night. It was minutes before he answered me. He slowly lifted his head to say yes. My heart pounded with fear for in a flash it dawned on me that Josh might be the one who murdered Ben. I asked him why he had left the house that night. He paused for a moment and gave a shy look as though he was ashamed of something. In a soft voice he said, "I went out of the house to use the toilet." Hearing this, any concerns or fear I had about him killing Ben vanished. Though I felt relieved by what he said, I again warned him about the severe consequences of going out of the house.

After weeks of ongoing mental and physical fatigue my health was in a state of decline and I had lost eleven pounds. Working at nights proved to be too tiring for me, so I decided to go back to my old routine of working the day shift.

Returning from work the following day, I noticed that some of the drawers of the kitchen cupboards were left partly open as though someone had been hurriedly searching for something. In the house there was an air of silence occasionally interrupted by the sound of dripping water from the leaky tap in the kitchen. Curious to find out what Josh was doing, I decided to visit him in the basement. I was taken by complete surprise to see Josh coming towards me with a large knife in his hand and a menacing look on his face. I became terrified and yelled at him to put away the knife. Afraid that he was going to attack me, I quickly turned and started to run back up the stairs, but he managed to grab me firmly by the hair. In fear, I surrendered and closed my eyes believing that he would kill me at any moment. As I imagined the sharp blade in his hand piercing into my stomach, I felt his hand letting go of my hair. I heard him say humbly: "Do not be afraid of me, I will not hurt you. You must put me to death so that I can return to the abode of the dead. I cannot commit suicide because my journey home would be long and full of sorrows. I have done you a favor by killing Ben while he was asleep and in return you must put me to death."

I realized that Josh was insane, and what had poisoned his mind was something I could not fully comprehend. Slowly opening my eyes, I said to him that I did not have the courage to kill anyone and he should put away the knife. My refusal greatly angered him and he became wild. With the knife clenched tightly in his hand he suddenly lunged at me. I quickly stepped back to prevent him from slashing me. In a flash I turned and ran out of the house, slamming the door in his face. I continued to run helter-skelter along the sidewalk, screaming for help. As I fearfully glanced over my shoulder I could not see Josh in pursuit of me, and with this I got a breath of relief. Surprisingly, he chose to remain in the house. I now realized that I had no choice but to get the police involved.

Later, several police officers arrived at my home. They surrounded the front of the house and began calling for Josh to come out. Realizing that he was not responding to their call, the police decided to storm through the front door and get him. But once inside they discovered that Josh could not be found anywhere. They hurried back outside to inform the others that he was not in the house and might have escaped through the open back door. To remove any suspicion that I had been secretly hiding Josh, I told the police that a short while ago he came to my home and threatened to kill me.

They now began a massive hunt for Josh in the surrounding area, but surprisingly no one could find him. The police decided to seek elsewhere and I was allowed to go back into the house. Being terribly afraid of Josh, I decided to search everywhere to ensure that he was not in the house. When I entered the basement I noticed that my outsized freezer was unplugged. I cautiously approached the freezer to open the door and became petrified by the horrifying sight of Josh sitting in the freezer with his knife pointed up at me. My heart pounded heavily from the sudden shock. My knees buckled and I could no longer stand up properly. I gently lowered myself at the side of the freezer and sat quietly on the floor in a state of defeat.

Josh stepped out of the freezer and got close to me. I felt helpless and closed my eyes, thinking my end was near. Instead, I felt a gentle touch on my shoulder and my body quivered. With my eyes still closed I then felt his arm around my shoulder. Softly he said, "You are the only one that I trust and I need your help. You must put me to death so that I may return to the abode of the dead."

I remained silent for a couple of minutes, thinking about my next move. I was afraid to call the police fearing that, in his rebellious frame of mind, the outcome would surely be a confrontation between the police and him. I slowly opened my eyes and said, "Tomorrow I will put you to death." What I said pleased him and immediately there was a change in his demeanor. He apologized for the way he had treated me and made it clear that apart from myself he disliked everyone on Earth for they had been unfair to him.

That night I could not sleep, knowing that Josh was resting in an adjacent room. Realizing how unpredictable he was, I felt afraid that he would force his way into my room at any moment and attack me. Now and again in this fearful night, he kept calling to remind me of the promise I had made to put him to death. It was not pleasant, for it seemed as though he was taunting me. Though I found this very annoying I decided to remain quiet and not disturb him in any way. At times I felt he was bored for I could hear him punching holes in the walls of his room with a knife and mumbling to himself. Through it all I decided to sit patiently awake on my bed until the break of dawn.

Early the next morning I heard him snoring heavily. Before leaving for work I decided to take my dog, Leo, for a walk. As I approached the doghouse I noticed that the lock and the hinges of the door had been ripped open. Strangely, there was no sound from the animal; normally upon seeing me, Leo would climb on his hind legs and bark through a small aperture above the kennel door.

When I opened the door of the pen I discovered that Leo was killed in a gruesome way. His neck was cut, and his tail and both ears were completely severed. After the grisly way Josh had killed Ben and his strange behavior, I had no doubt that Josh had killed the dog. I now realized that I was harboring a dangerous man who seemed to have a thirst for blood. After a short deliberation I decided to remain silent about the killing of the dog, believing that if I accused Josh he would turn violent.

Returning to the house, I quickly got dressed and left for work while Josh was still asleep. At the hospital I learned from the local newspaper about a nation-wide hunt for Josh. Knowing how much he wanted to die and the mental torture he would continue to experience if alive, I decided not to inform the police. Having made a promise to put him to death painlessly, I secretly stole a deadly drug from the hospital that could kill him in a very short time.

Throughout the day it was difficult for me to remain focused because my mind was in a state of muddle. When reflecting upon the earlier circumstances that poisoned Josh's mind, it became very distressing to keep harboring the thought of killing someone like him.

On my way home from work it suddenly dawned upon me that if Josh was put to death, Maria would have to spend the rest of her life in prison since I would be removing the only piece of evidence that could possibly set her free. In order for her to be released, Josh would have to admit removing the life support devices of those patients who had died. On the other hand I could not bear the thought of Josh being sent to prison for murder, knowing that his real intention was only to set those patients free and not to kill them. I knew that he was totally unaware of the importance of their life support devices.

With these conflicting views constantly filtering through my mind, I realized that my life could become one of sorrow and guilt. Strangely, I was beginning to think that Maria's only intention might have been to set Josh free and not for him to remove the life support from those patients. However, I still had my doubts about Maria because I could not fully comprehend what she had in mind in setting Josh free.

The decision to either put Josh to death or help Maria was a difficult one to make, and I could not say if I had made the right choice. The compassionate feelings I had for Josh were overpowering, and in this troubled frame of mind I decided to keep my promise and put him to death. Fearing that I might lose courage with further deliberation, I decided to end his life as soon as I got home.

When I returned from work that day I was eager to find Josh. With a strong intention to put him to death, my feelings of compassion changed into distrust and resentment. In haste I led Josh by the hand into the basement and told him to sit on a chair close to the freezer. I then took out the deadly drug hidden in my purse and injected it into his shoulder. In a matter of seconds his face frowned with emotions and tears flowed from his eyes. Before he could move his hands to wipe the teardrops, his eyes suddenly closed and he was completely gone. His death was short and painless, for it only took ninety seconds for his heart to stop beating.

I became totally confused as the thought of being charged and imprisoned for life raced through my mind. With no prior plans of how to get rid of the dead body I became nervous and frightened. Fearing the harsh consequences to follow, I decided not to disclose to anyone what I had done. As a religious person I felt that I had betrayed God by committing a terrible sin. Amid all these feelings, I realized that even though my mind was in a state of torment, I had to think quickly of a way to extricate myself from this quandary.

I decided to hide the dead body in the freezer. With a great deal of effort I managed to move his lifeless body to lean against the open unit. I then grabbed him by his feet and tossed him into the freezer. I realized that there was something suspicious about the way his crouched body was positioned, so I quickly maneuvered him around to make him sit in an upright position. I hurriedly placed some frozen meat around him to make it look as if he had squeezed himself into the freezer. I then shut the door and put the power back on.

Turning my thoughts away from God, I began to think of ways to free myself from being charged for murder. After some deliberation I decided to get the police involved in a way that would make me look innocent and eliminate me as a suspect in this killing.

Early the next morning I left quietly for work. On my way out I saw a couple of policemen sitting in their parked vehicle approximately thirty meters away from my home. I could only guess they were there to protect me from Josh whom they suspected might come back to visit me.

When I returned from work later that day, I hurriedly went down into the basement and opened the door of the freezer. I reached out to touch Josh and felt his body, frozen like a rock. I quickly got on the phone to inform the police that I had found Josh's dead body inside the freezer. Within minutes the police arrived at my home and immediately began questioning me on how I had discovered the body. I told them that I had just returned from work, and upon opening the freezer to take out some meat to prepare dinner, I discovered the dead body. After that they questioned me no further, realizing that when they came into my house looking for Josh, they had never searched inside the freezer. Josh's frozen body was later removed from the house by paramedics and taken to determine the true cause of death.

In days to follow nothing was disclosed to the public about the Cryonic Man's autopsy or plans to dispose of his body. Knowing the technological skill of these scientists and the determination they had to keep this man alive, I could not resist the thought of them wanting to bring him back to life a second time. However, I doubted they could bring him back to life, knowing the serious effect of the deadly drug that I had injected into his body.

But only two weeks after Josh's death I heard the astonishing news on the radio that the Cryonic Man was momentarily brought back to life by scientists. This greatly angered me for I could not comprehend why they did this knowing how much he had suffered on Earth. I gathered from what was said on the news that on this occasion, he died from shock after being brought back to life and seeing himself surrounded by doctors. To him it was like waking up suddenly from a horrifying dream only to discover that it was real and happening at that moment. In the end his weak heart could no longer respond to any form of treatment.

In the coming months no one questioned me about Josh. For unknown reasons, the cause of his death prior to the second attempt to bring him back to life was kept secret. I decided to remain silent about the matter and hoped not to be caught.

Like Josh, my life too seemed doleful in having to experience so many unfortunate things so frequently. As the days went by I began to think more and more about the murder I had committed, and I started to develop a feeling of guilt. Having strong religious values, I felt I had betrayed the Lord by sinning.

In days to follow, the feeling of guilt became unbearable, so I decided to undergo psychotherapy in the hope that it would lessen my burden. During the therapy I remained silent and never disclosed to the doctor the nature of the crime I had committed. I soon realized that this would make it difficult for him to fully analyze my situation. Instead of feeling better with therapy I began to sink further into depression. After weeks of being constantly advised and told what to do, I was losing confidence in myself. I developed a strange feeling that, in seeking help of this nature, something was wrong with me mentally and I was not a normal person.

Amid this distress I decided to stop being advised and turned to the Lord for redemption. I began to pray sincerely to God to show me a way to free myself from sorrow. Soon the local church that I had attended for a number of years came to mind, and I decided to go there for comfort. Listening to the enchanting hymns in church and hearing our local priest, Mr. Benny Barclay, glorify the name of God not only provided me with a change of heart but calmed my restless mind as well.

During a special church service one Sunday, I heard a very touching and inspiring speech by Mr. Barclay. I always thought of him as a humble, courteous and well-mannered person. Every time I saw him in public or in church he was very well-dressed and had his hair neatly groomed. He was greatly respected by everyone who attended church because of the sound and professional advice he gave to those who were in distress.

During the service he talked about the greatness of God and the love the Lord has for those who seek peace and forgiveness. When he spoke of repentance I became deeply emotional and wept. Being a sinner seeking forgiveness, I could no longer control my feelings of guilt.

When the sermon was over, I sat alone in church and uttered a silent prayer seeking clemency from God. I got up nervously and picked up my handbag in preparation to leave. As I walked slowly along the corridor, I was approached by Mr. Barclay who politely asked why I looked so dejected. I could only guess he must have seen me crying during the sermon. I tried to elude him by telling him everything was well with me, but then he began to encourage me to confide in him. In this place of worship I realized that I could not lie or conceal the truth, and with this made a full confession. I recounted to him the whole story about Josh and how I had killed him. I felt mentally relieved for a short while, and for some reason I got the false feeling that this was probably the end of my feelings of guilt. However, Mr. Barclay then began a lengthy talk with me. He spoke to me persuasively about truth and the importance of the law. Listening to what he said, I became emotional once more and began to cry. Kindly he indicated that he could not harbor me as a criminal and that I should turn myself over to the law. What he said made me totally distraught for I was not prepared to deal with the harsh consequences of my actions for killing someone. Then Mr. Barclay said to me that what I was going to experience would be distressing, but through it all I should never lose faith in God.

Having given me what seemed to be the best piece of advice, Mr. Barclay then told me not to leave immediately for he had something confidential to tell me. I prepared myself mentally to listen to something that was not related to the church.

However, what he had to say was appalling and unbelievable, and for a moment I was left with my mouth agape. Mr. Barclay, fully dressed in white clothing, confessed to me that he had been unfaithful to his wife by having an extra-marital affair with my sister June. A worried look was on his face as if he deeply regretted his involvement with June. Seconds later, I thought he was going to break down and cry when I saw him reaching into his pocket to take out his handkerchief, but he suddenly sneezed and then began to wipe his nose.

Throughout our conversation he spoke with his head down as though he was terribly ashamed to look at me in the face. In remorse, he went on to say that the relationship he was having with my sister had only ended two months ago when he discovered that June had been swindling church followers by taking money offered as donations for her own personal use.

Seeing that Mr. Barclay was open to confessing what he had done, I questioned him about how he got involved with June. Without hesitation he told me that his wife became sickly and was later confined to a bed as her health worsened. And after tending to her for quite some time, he grew tired and frustrated. He claimed that one Sunday after the church service had ended, my sister June came over to visit his sickly wife and became deeply touched by what she saw.

June was considerate and, of her own accord, volunteered to visit his home three times a week to assist him in taking care of his suffering wife. After a couple of months a love affair developed between June and himself. And soon, he was having an extramarital relationship with June while his wife was still sick in bed.

Mr. Barclay went on to say that later, June told him that his wife might not live much longer and she was hoping that after her death the two of them would marry. In a short time June became obsessed with the luxurious home of his wife and began to act like the true mistress of the house. She strongly believed that after the death of his wife, he would be the one to inherit all the wealth, and she would be the one he would share it with.

June, realizing that his wife was not dying as soon as she expected, grew frustrated. Her mind became poisoned with greed and money became the most important thing to her. Driven by further desire to get rich, she then started to steal from the church. In spite of his warning her about the wrong she was doing, she still kept misusing the money that was given to her in trust by supporters of the church. Wanting to look young and attractive, June began spending thousands of dollars on fashionable clothing, make-up and perfumes.

I also learned during our conversation that Mr. Barclay was a simple man who was married to a woman who had inherited a great deal of wealth from her parents. Through the generosity and support of his wife, he was able to offer large sums of her money to the construction of the local church. When his wife was in good health she used to attend the church regularly, until fellow church members began to gossip about her after she refused to offer more of her own money towards the expansion of the church. Some members were jealous of his wife's wealth and, not getting what they wanted, began to speak of her money as evil.

After his wife had stopped attending the church, the gossip lessened and eventually faded away when they all learned of her illness. Shortly afterward, a group of church members, including my sister June, started a special fund to raise money for the expansion of the church. June was chosen by members of the church to take care of all collections and to handle all financial matters. Given this assignment that required honesty and trust, June went astray and began siphoning the money for her own personal use.

Mr. Barclay claimed that what made matters worse and caused their relationship to turn sour was June becoming less attentive to his wife and treating her in an unfriendly manner. She became unwilling to serve her food in bed and to give her the daily medication that was prescribed by doctors.

Listening to all these negative things about my sister was disheartening. Amid his reproach I felt driven by my own instincts to say something in her defense. Most of what Mr. Barclay said seemed rather one-sided, for it appeared as though June was completely at fault. I could not say whether he was trying to save himself from shame or trying to protect his own credibility. To test his sincerity I politely asked him if he had at any time during their relationship made a promise to marry my sister. I suspected that, in order for June to begin acting like his wife or the mistress of the house, he might have made such a promise. Hearing this question, he appeared stunned and looked upwards to the ceiling of the church, perhaps in search of an answer. Mr. Barclay could not answer this question and simply remained silent about it. To avoid any further discussion on this subject, he politely said that it was time for him to leave, as he had to return home to his ailing wife. His reluctance to answer my question left me in doubt for I could not know if he was telling the whole truth. I felt that his entire love affair with June was ignominious and he might have to suffer the consequences of his actions.

Mr. Barclay's affair with my sister disturbed me greatly. I knew from the beginning that June had a desire to marry someone who was rich and righteous. However, it was difficult to believe that the righteous one she chose had to be a married preacher! For a moment, though adultery seemed the lesser of the two evils, I began to reflect more upon my own sister stealing from a place of worship.

Seeing how remorseful Mr. Barclay was about his relationship with June, I became a little sympathetic towards him for it seemed as though he had made one terrible mistake and deeply regretted it. It was sad to see so elegant a man, with excellent manners, fall to disgrace when he swerved from his religious teachings.

I decided to visit June to find out the truth. I did not want to accuse her wrongly for something that she might not have done. When I arrived at her home she looked pleased and welcomed me with lots of hugs and kisses. I was very cold in accepting her greetings after hearing so many disturbing things about her. My stay at her home was very short, for I questioned her immediately about what Mr. Barclay said about her stealing from the church and insisted that she speak the truth. June confessed that she was indeed stealing from the church. Totally outraged, I immediately left her home and never looked back to say goodbye. In my anger I completely forgot to ask her if she had had a love affair with Mr. Barclay. I assumed without hearing any further from her that she was involved with the priest.

On my way home, thinking about what Mr. Barclay said to me earlier about the importance of the law became instilled in my mind. His views certainly altered the way I looked upon the law, for in the past I rarely reflected on how effective it could be in controlling evil.

I began to think of my duty to uphold the law. I could not comprehend what caused my sister to swerve from the path of righteousness to that of evil. My only guess was that she must have attached too much importance to the way she looked and appealed to others. As a middle-aged woman she seemed to become too absorbed in the modern changes of people's attitudes in trying to stay fit, desirable and beautiful. With so much external influence, as well as her own narcissism, she became distracted with fantasy and swerved away from reality. In analyzing all that had happened to her, I felt convinced that her reputation would be ruined and she might have to live in shame.

With a new belief in upholding the law, I felt that even though June was my own sister I had to sever our sisterly relationship so as to put an end to the evil things she was doing. I could not bear the thought of her swindling innocent people. After a short deliberation I decided to be an informant and notify the police about the embezzlement.

What became of June after I had informed the police would remain unknown to me, for after having reported the matter I immediately began to reflect upon my own wrong doings. I began making my own plans to inform the police about the murder I had committed.

CHAPTER 5

It was at the break of dawn when I wiped my weary eyes and got out of bed to open the curtains to allow the sunlight into my room. As I watched the shining rays of the sun emerge out of the dark clouds, I began to think of the elements of the natural world and the beauty that emerges from it all. For many who dwell in it, life seems to be a wonderful experience when most things work to their advantage, and they are not greatly affected by periods of misfortune. Life for me has never been like that. Filled with adversity, my life seems to be a sad and stressful experience with sporadic moments of joy. Amid these distraught feelings I began to reflect upon the confessions that I had made to Mr. Barclay and what he had advised me to do. Unable to cope with guilt, I decided to inform the police about the killing of Josh.

My confession to this murder was shocking, especially to those who attended the local church, for they found it difficult to believe that I could take someone's life. Within days I was summoned to appear in court to stand trial for the murder of Josh. This was worrisome for me since I had to reiterate in court details of how I had committed the homicide.

After the trial, I developed mixed feelings about what I had confessed to. I was sentenced to thirty-five years of incarceration, so telling the truth proved not to be rewarding for me, because I now had to face the harsh consequences of my actions. For a while it was an unhappy period in my life, but slowly, I began to accept my imprisonment since I realized there was nothing I could do to change things. With time I became more poised and fulfilled from telling the truth. And as a religious person I honestly felt good about it, for my feelings of guilt began to diminish slowly.

Approximately six months later I was transferred to a secluded and heavily guarded government penitentiary. In the prison compound I saw Maria who was serving a similar prison sentence. As I stared at her from a distance, I developed a feeling of loathing, believing that her intentions were immoral when planning to set Josh free. I felt that, being in favor of euthanasia, she somehow toyed with his emotions and lured him into killing those patients, without his understanding the fatality of his actions.

At this new location I was escorted by prison guards to a cell for two. A few hours later I became extremely irritated when I saw Maria being brought in to share the same cell with me. In a fit of anger I shouted at the guards to get her out of my cell, but before I could say anything further one of the guards yelled at me to shut up! I realized that in prison I had no choice but to do as I was told.

It was not a pleasant feeling to be locked in prison with someone I disliked. The two of us sat at opposite ends of the room for almost an hour before Maria broke the silence. She told me that we were both in the same predicament and there was no need for us to keep on harboring ill feelings for each other.

Still annoyed with her, I rudely said, "Why did you encourage Josh to murder those patients?" In reply, Maria flatly denied having anything to do with the killings. She claimed that she shared the same compassionate feelings as I had for Josh, and she did not like the inhumane way he was being treated in hospital. She said that all she ever wanted was to free Josh, and she had no idea that he was going to remove the life support devices from those patients.

She claimed that after witnessing the mental torture Josh had endured, she realized that a hundred years was too long before being restored to life. She felt that, since Josh had no relatives or friends, and no knowledge of what was required to survive in a modern world, he was at a serious disadvantage. Apart from these heart-felt expressions, she claimed that in some cases she still supported the idea of bringing someone back to life, especially if their body was in a healthy state at the time of death, and if a cure is found several years later. She explained that, even though she knew what Josh had done was wrong, she tried to protect him by declaring that she was the killer.

This made me less angry for I realized that there was some truth in her story. Since I had killed Josh who could have borne testimony to what truly happened, I now realized that there was no hope for Maria ever being set free.

In prison, Maria and I shared the same cell, and as inmates both of us realized that we were in the same predicament. In confinement, amity was necessary to ease the feelings of loneliness, so we renewed our friendship.

As the years in prison progressed, religious studies became of interest to me as they kept my mind active with a desire to gain knowledge about God. Maria, on the other hand, was not interested in the teachings from the scriptures since she had doubts about God ever helping her while in prison. But with time, she became a better person as she grew less arrogant and less loquacious.

Sadly, after fourteen years in prison she developed a severe case of pneumonia and died. As a prisoner, she was not given the best of medical attention, as the prison officials paid little attention to her health. She lay sick in bed for four days before receiving medical help, and would only live to spend one night in hospital before passing away.

During her illness I told her several times how much I prayed to God for her to get better for I strongly believed in the power of prayer. I was very surprised when Maria told me that my prayers would not cure her illness and I should seek medical help for her. She told me that prayer is something to comfort people in their sorrows and to keep them identifying with God and all that is virtuous. The only one she believed could cure her was a medical doctor, for in her beliefs God will work mysteriously through a doctor's efforts to help her.

Maria's death was a sad and memorable one. Fearing death during her illness, she asked one question, "Why do I, Maria, have to die?"

Before answering I paused for a moment to think, and then humbly said, "All that happens and results in death is the manifestation of an indisputable universal law in which all that is born must die." I told her that life did not end with the death of her physical body because her thoughts or true self never dies since it is imperishable.

Maria and I had a sisterly relationship for over fourteen years and during this time I had become closely attached to her. Our separation by death was a period of great sadness. Being confined to a prison cell and dwelling in idleness, I found it difficult not to think about her each day. I began to experience sleepless nights as I lamented constantly over her sudden illness and death. Then I began to question my own religious beliefs as to why a caring and respectable person like Maria should suffer with severe illness and die. With no friends or relatives to comfort or support me in this time of grief, I realized that I had to struggle in isolation to get rid of these discouraging feelings. Afraid of falling into a state of depression, I tried to harbor only pleasant thoughts about Maria. I started to reminisce about the good times that we shared together and to think of her as a decent and loving human being. Surprisingly, when I did this there was a major change in me as I began to have pleasant dreams about Maria. With images of her in my mind I tried to tell her that my love for her would never die and she would live forever in my heart. These affectionate feelings, however, were ephemeral for in days to follow I realized that what I was experiencing was not real. For, on waking up from sleep and witnessing Maria's bed empty, I would fall into despair. Once again, I began to experience those dark and depressing feelings.

Realizing that my emotional state was gradually worsening, I began to think of ways to extricate myself from sorrow. When I had practically lost all hope, my religious beliefs gave me the strength to cope with bereavement. It dawned on me that I was not the only one who suffered grief, as others too had experienced a similar loss. I now realized that I had to learn how to cope with the sorrowful experience of death. Reflecting upon the universal and indisputable law in which all that is born must die, I came to appreciate the immense value of religion in times of disconsolation. Amidst my sorrows, my religious beliefs gave me comfort and strength to accept the death of this loved one. It was here in prison that I wrote the story of my life to share some of my experiences and thoughts.

Over the years I believed that if I lived a righteous life I would reap the benefits of my good deeds, but unfortunately I never got any form of earthly rewards for doing good. It took the death of a loved one for me to realize that it was not judicious to seek after any rewards for the pious acts I perform. For death is unstoppable and can happen any day. I now realized that it was useless for me to seek after something that might never come.

After the untimely death of Maria, my desire for earthly rewards changed as I now began to think of an after-life reward for doing good. With this in mind I began to question myself about what happens to a person when he or she dies. I spent hours pondering on this question but never found anything that could substantiate what happens after death. It seemed to be a mystery, as I could only speculate and hope that the deceased would find an abode of peace and joy.

As an elderly person I feel that, by not knowing what happens after death, my mind remains on a path of progressive development. In the case of the Cryonic Man I feel confident that one's true self never dies, for after a hundred years he could still talk about his after-death experiences which were similar to that of a dream. If I knew what happened after death and discovered that I did not like it, then this would certainly leave my mind in a state of torment as I would rather not die. On the other hand, if everyone learned that life after death was something far better than what they experienced on Earth, then they might choose to die. In analyzing it all, I feel that I am fortunate to experience life on Earth whether it be long, short, good or bad. For there is more to learn in two separate experiences than one. In taking on a human body I could experience joy and suffering, and through it all I was able to reflect on my beliefs and to speculate on the next phase of life.

In comparing my way of life to that of Maria's I felt that, even though she lived a short life, the things she experienced and accomplished were enormous. She achieved a great deal more in her short life than me because of the number of things she accomplished and enjoyed in her active lifestyle. Maria once said to me that as a teenager she had a strong desire to learn different things and to become successful in a number of ways. Apart from her interests in science and law, she was adventurous. She visited many distant lands to meet people from all walks of life and learn about their ways. She loved and enjoyed the company of her relatives and friends in social gatherings, even though I often heard her talk openly about the number of arguments she had had with people over trivial matters. Because she was so talkative and persistent about her beliefs, she often found herself in conflict with others. In spite of this, Maria found the time for reconciliation and would never harbor ill feelings for anyone for a long period of time. In short, for a single day she could be your worst enemy and on the next your best friend.

In contrast to Maria, I was too reticent and rarely took part in social gatherings or festivities because I was too absorbed with my religious beliefs and concerns for ethics. While I spent a great deal of my time agonizing over my sorrowful experiences, Maria kept herself busy with a number of prison activities. Though she was incarcerated, she never allowed herself to become weakened by emotions for she kept thinking about the positive aspects of life. Because of her academic skills, she was allowed to tutor prisoners on a number of subjects. And to ease the mental stress of living in seclusion, she even took part in organizing recreational activities for prisoners.

In solitude, I have often questioned myself about what it is that I need from life. I have never been able to answer this question truthfully because at each phase of my life my desires change. With everything that I chose to do, it appears that I was driven by desire to perform actions, with little or no time to reflect upon them. As a teenager it was my ambition to become a qualified nurse, and having achieved this, it seemed I had been performing a daily routine that was necessary for me to survive in a world where money determined my standard of living. It seemed to me that everyone is moved to perform actions in some form or other for their own survival. Action in one way or another appears to be involved in everything, whether it is breathing, thinking, acts of nature or the disintegration of things. With such thoughts in mind, I am drawn to believe that everything that is driven into action may be a part of a Single Infinite One which exists by performing perpetual action. Action seems to be the thing that keeps the universe alive and without it everything may become meaningless or cease to exist.

Despite all the righteous actions that I had performed in the early stages of my marriage, I could not honestly say that they were all pious acts, for the more I reflect on it, the more I am inclined to believe that some of these acts were not judicious. As a young woman I dedicated a great deal of time to acts of benevolence, assisting and giving generously to the poor. I believed in and worshipped God with implicit faith and prayed to become divinely enlightened. To those who had repeatedly done wrong I was sympathetic and hoped that they would change for the better. I was against punishing anyone harshly for serious crimes for I believed in edification and reformation of the offender. My husband Jim had always warned me not to be too much of a timid or caring person because others would take advantage of me. It was not until Jim was murdered that my beliefs changed and the importance of the law came to mind. From this, I began to ask myself whether I had been blindly compassionate and had paid little attention to fairness. I soon realized that some of my actions which I considered good might in fact not be, for what is the point of being too compassionate to evil doers and ignoring those who suffer from their ungodly actions? As I reflect upon some of the unfortunate things that happened to me, I feel drawn to believe that, because of the way I think and the decisions I made, I am partially responsible for some of my own sufferings.

Maria, on the other hand, was less compassionate and forgiving than I. She was a stern woman who believed in respect for the law, but felt it would never be perfect in its entirety. She spoke out openly against certain technicalities or flaws in the law, wanting them overruled or recommended for immediate change during a court trial. This, she believed, would prevent notorious criminals and celebrities from being acquitted or given a lesser prison sentence due to public sympathy or loopholes in the law.

Apart from having these virtues, Maria was assertive, educated and eloquent in speech. People for various reasons respected her more than me. It appeared that all the righteous things I had done were only remembered for a short period and might be equally important as Maria's beliefs in upholding the law. Unlike the series of misfortunes I had encountered, life for the greater part had been good to Maria for she was never faced with any serious form of adversity prior to her conviction. I could not say whether it was good luck, her beliefs or her way of thinking that made life less of a sorrowful experience than I had encountered. I have often suspected myself of being too absorbed in doing good, and not analyzing carefully the effects of my actions. I felt inclined to believe that even what I considered to be good, such as humility, is questionable. For what is the point of allowing the evil doers to take advantage of me, and not making any attempt to stop it through a belief in fairness and justice?

Now that I have grown old, thinking about death, which I rarely did when I was young, begins to fill my mind. In this final stage of my life I am able to discover how my desires change, as I feel drawn to be less sociable. In a way detachment seems to be slowly bringing a little comfort to me as I feel the need to be more by myself. Though at times I feel the necessity for a little kindness or a helping hand from others, in a humble way I prefer to be silent and not burden others with my problems.

In a world that exists outside these prison walls, I can imagine a new generation of infants born to take the place of those who have passed away, in a cycle that appears continuous and that sets the human mind on a path of progressive development. Though my life for the greater part has been filled with sorrow, I remain pleased that I have not swerved away from my belief in that Infinite One called God.

THE TRUE SELF

CHAPTER I

It was 5:30 p.m. and Dusty Mills opened his eyes just as he was about to be buried. From the murky sky there was a tumultuous roar of thunder and a fierce discharge of lightning that momentarily set the sky alight. It was as if something cataclysmic was about to happen. The glistening light made him fully awake as he winked his watery eyes and frowned. Slowly, he slid open the coffin cover, then extended his arm outward and showed a tightly clenched fist, perhaps to express his anger. The funeral attendants gasped aloud. His mud-crusted face and bulging red eyes made him look terrifying.

Surrounded by hundreds of mourners dressed in black, the man who rose from the dead thought he was in hell. He now became afraid of the living and saw them as the angels of death. However, the funeral attendants were more fearful of the dead rising and took to their heels, leaving him totally disoriented.

He got up and stood motionless for a minute with both hands held stiffly by his side and his neck partially withdrawn into his broad shoulders. He was frozen with fear. The expression on his face seemed as if he were in dire need of help. With his mouth agape, he then looked down in total shock to see himself standing in a black wooden coffin, lined with white rags and no pillow. In dismay, he moved his hand slowly and touched the only symbol of reverence, which was a golden crucifix he always wore around his neck.

The rotten scent of decaying flesh caused him to look anxiously around in greater fear, not knowing that this place for interment was an isolated, pest-infested waste dump where, some twenty meters away, a flock of hungry vultures was pecking furiously at the flesh of a dead animal. As he looked upward he was puzzled by the sight of a teenage boy named Matthew who stood smiling down at the coffin. Seeing the lad he became a little more poised and in a coarse voice said, "I am thirsty, fetch me some water." The lad, filled with enthusiasm, ran quickly to bring him a jug of water. Realizing that Dusty was too weak to climb out of the hole, young Matthew carefully lowered himself into it to give him the water.

After drinking, Dusty Mills licked his lips, which had dry pieces of mud stuck on them. He then rubbed his stomach and made a sickening belch as if he were experiencing some minor discomfort. Looking at him straight in the face, Matthew could see that his nostrils were clogged with pieces of mud which seemed to obstruct his breathing. Though he looked dreadful, Matthew seemed unaffected. He was too pleased to see the man alive.

Matthew, realizing that Dusty was nervous and shaky and unable to stand properly, carefully maneuvered the big man around so as to close the empty coffin. Together they sat down on top of the coffin with Dusty looking very disconcerted. Young Matthew, however, was still exhilarated knowing that he was alive. This was probably the greatest moment in his life, for he strongly believed that the Lord had answered his prayer in bringing Dusty Mills back to life.

Looking at Dusty's mud-crusted face, Matthew showed compassion and began to wash it with the remaining water. As the dirt came off, he was astonished to see that there were no longer any unpleasant sores on Dusty's face. He even noticed that his eyes had become normal. When Matthew told him about this, an exuberant Dusty Mills smiled in delight. With renewed feelings, he eagerly placed his hands over his face, gently rubbing it to ensure what Matthew said was true. He could not fully comprehend what had happened and in a soft tone of voice asked, "Why was I put in a coffin?"

In reply, Matthew briefly recounted the events that led to Dusty Mills being taken for burial. He indicated that Dusty was very much hated in the village of Hadeson because of his violent behavior. And, like everyone else, he too had grown tired of Dusty's evil actions and wanted to put an end to them. Matthew explained that one day he waited in ambush while Dusty was on his knees taking an oath to God, cautiously approached him from behind and dealt him a severe blow to the head with a rock. Immediately Dusty fell to the ground unconscious. Many villagers, peeking from their windows, saw the incident and quickly ran out of their homes to look at the injured man who lay motionless.

The villagers looked pleased as they watched the man who had terrorized them lie helplessly on the ground. They began deliberating over how to get him out of their neighborhood. However, everyone became concerned when they realized that Dusty Mills was failing to regain consciousness. What remained puzzling to them was that his eyes were fully open, but there was no movement from any part of his body. Soon, a decision was made to take the inert man back to the old farmhouse where he lived.

Twenty-four hours later something strange occurred. They noticed that his eyes had spontaneously shut although he remained unconscious. With no more fear of Dusty Mills, some of the villagers began to treat his body with disrespect. They began twisting and turning his arms and legs roughly to see if he would wake up. There was some degree of uncertainty over this prone body. One of the villagers even put his head on Dusty's chest to listen for a heartbeat while others attempted to open his eyes with their fingers. Observing no movement from Dusty, an elder declared him dead and ordered burial for the following day. The villagers concurred and, the next day, Dusty was taken to a special place for interment.

Everyone gathered around the wooden coffin with a small opening at the top. Through this small window, the unpleasant face of Dusty Mills could be seen. The majority were superstitious, and with their coarse voices and different forms of gesticulation, whatever they did seemed more of an incantation. They being entrenched in their beliefs, Matthew was doubtful of them ever changing their way of life that clung to tradition. They felt that evil might fall upon them if they did not adhere to their ancestral beliefs.

As Dusty's coffin was lowered into the hole, young Matthew explained that he became filled with pity when he realized that he was responsible for this death. The psychological effects of killing someone and having to perform part of his funeral rites were too poignant for him. Tearfully, he prayed: "O Lord, forgive me for killing this man. I do not want to live in sin or with guilt. Please Lord, I promise to serve Thee forever if this man is brought back to life."

Finally, the moment came when people began to throw pieces of soil on top of the coffin with the intention of covering it. Suddenly, a revengeful and frustrated man angrily kicked a huge piece of hardened mud into the hole, striking the coffin with a loud bang. Just then, young Matthew explained, he saw the eyes of Dusty open wide. With a frantic cry, he shouted, "He is alive! He is alive!" Apparently, Dusty had fallen into a coma and, with the sudden bang on the coffin, he had regained consciousness.

Moments later, everyone saw the hands of Dusty Mills push open the cover of the coffin. His fingers were covered with dry clay and had the shape of an eagle's claw, about to snatch its prey. It was a grisly scene for the local villagers who began to scream and run wildly across the burial site. They hurried home, fearing the devil was upon them. Witnessing this, Matthew's heart pounded with excitement. He felt that this was a miracle and there was no need to run away, for the Lord had answered his prayer by bringing the man back to life.

Looking regretful, he apologized to Dusty for striking him. With special emphasis, he told Dusty how he had lain motionless for one day with his eyes open, but on the second day, everyone thought he had finally died because his eyes suddenly closed while the rest of his body remained inert.

Dusty Mills listened attentively to what Matthew had to say and then politely said, "Stay with me for a while and I will tell you the reason for my ungodly behavior and about a place that I have visited far beyond the earth."

The scene of two people sitting on top of a coffin six feet below the earth's surface was almost surreal. Here, one of the most astonishing stories ever told would unfold. Dusty, looking much more composed, slowly began to rub his eyes and, as he did this, the recollection of an incredible journey began to filter through his mind. He came to be reacquainted with himself and began to recollect the incidents of his life…

CHAPTER 2

On a hazy Sunday afternoon, the last train bound for Georgia arrived at the station. While scores of commuters were eager to get on the train, others took a little extra time to bid farewell to their relatives and friends. Through the large crowd of people I hurriedly pushed my way to assist an elderly woman to board. Amongst the noisy crowd an angry person yelled, "You son of a bitch!" Evidently, I had inadvertently stepped on someone's toes. I was a professional con man, who happened to be late on this occasion in bidding farewell to another one of my victims. I had just tricked this elderly woman out of her savings and was eager to see her leave.

As the train slowly heaved out of the station, the elderly woman waved good-bye to me, not knowing that she had been cheated by someone she trusted. I had no intention of earning an honest living, so I smiled in relief and began to think of my next move to become rich and famous. I was up-to-date with current affairs since I read and watched the news daily, and this was a part of the astute strategy that I used to track down my prey.

The reason I had chosen the path of unrighteousness is that I observed how easily people could be deceived, and because of my dualistic view of good and evil. By virtue of what I learnt from the disparity between right and wrong, I was able to develop my thinking and understand a oneness which encompasses both of them. In my view, if everyone strove to become good like sages and not be a part of what furthers the economic growth of a society, then our world would become filled with roaming beggars. Much of what is considered evil seems to make life interesting for me, as I am able to have fun and to prosper in life. Some of the things that I considered bad, such as being rejected or disappointed in not getting what I desired, often proved to be good or beneficial to me, for on several occasions I narrowly escaped being accused or charged with fraud. If I am ever brought to justice I will encounter sorrow while the righteous may rejoice, therefore good and evil are a part of life's experiences. While many who were industrious and caring suffer mental stress in agonizing over the things that displeased them, I kept my mind occupied with pleasant thoughts on how to enjoy the fruits of their good actions.

In an age when technology had reached its culminating point, many with a great deal of technological skills no longer found any challenge in their occupation since there was little left to explore or develop in computers which provided artificial intelligence. Surprisingly, the subject of utmost interest to many scientists was genetic engineering. They began to understand more clearly the nature of biological inheritance and how human characteristics are passed on from parent to offspring. Though the quality of human life was greatly improved by these scientific achievements, this field had its limitations because certain experiments were ethically inadmissible. Many feared that if genetics was misused it could disrupt the harmony of things. When speculation began regarding the origin of the gene, many intellectuals came to believe that all living things evolved out of nature, and the universe itself is the single source of everything. While many view genetic engineering as a threat to religious beliefs, others envision the coming of something good from what was considered bad. Many foresee this branch of science greatly reducing the spread of same-sex relationships, as well as discovering a cure for severe neurosis and the prevention of hundreds of diseases in human beings, plants and animals.

As some branches of science rapidly rose to the pinnacle of success, others lost momentum. One such example was the longevity of life recently achieved through medical research in the field of gerontology. This scientific break-through slowed down the process of aging.

In many ways people became bored and frustrated with life. Longevity became a desire for many who believed that immortality could be achieved. However, they failed to realize that with this psychological resistance to age and decay, the human mind became restless as it constantly had to adapt to the process of change.

For those who remained composed, life had a more meaningful purpose as they turned to a new branch of study which sought to explain the nature of the universe. They happened to be only a small minority of people as the masses still had to face the harsh reality of how to survive in a country where the majority was burdened by financial debt. While many sought after wealth and knowledge, I spent my leisure time thinking of ways to swindle them.

I realized that people of the middle class were over-stressed by a growing pessimism about their future. In a system where borrowing money was encouraged, many struggled for the greater part of their lives to pay back huge loans. With the cost of living on the rise, and almost everyone being highly taxed on whatever they earned or possessed, people were pressured into working harder to keep up with the social and economic changes. In such a relentless environment many people grew to dislike their occupations since whatever they earned seemed not enough to provide them with the things they desired. These conditions caused many to become disgruntled.

I noticed that whenever a violent criminal was put on trial, public sympathy would often be for the criminal rather than for the innocent victim. And I observed how the bureaucracy had become too focused in maintaining those laws which brought in revenue for the government. With this in mind, I avoided breaking laws related to taxation or serious traffic violations because the authorities often acted swiftly in imposing fines. Instead, I targeted the overstressed and hard-working citizens by swindling them of their savings. In my view, the law was getting weaker, for crimes of a more serious nature often lost their momentum due to lengthy trials. This resulted in shorter prison sentences for criminals or in the offense being treated as a misdemeanor.

I discovered that a large proportion of the population had a thirst for gossip, false promises, and an insatiable appetite for salacious material about the rich and the famous. These conditions were very encouraging for me and I felt that the time was right to capitalize on these human frailties. Carefully analyzing these problems, I decided that on the political level I would be the voice of the middle class and, for the poor, I would be the preacher who would comfort them in their sorrows. There was a growing trend among people to become followers and believers of whatever they saw the majority saying or doing. And I realized how anxious people were to hear promises made by prominent leaders of society. Lies and false promises seemed to have become the political strategies used by politicians to gain status.

Keeping these thoughts in mind, I decided to become both a political candidate in the national elections and a religious preacher. Using false credentials and bribery, I soon found myself in the company of the elite and respected members of society. As a result, I posed endlessly before the press cameras, shaking the hands of the poor and the deprived. Using the rhetoric of other successful candidates in the past, I promised everything possible to better their lives. Many who saw me visiting the sick and the homeless believed I was compassionate and placed their confidence in me. I admonished those who were distressed and had turned to religion as a source of comfort to have faith in the Lord, for they would be cured of their illness and granted a place in heaven. With the financial support I received from these followers, I was able to enjoy a life of luxury. Away from the campaign trail and in secret meeting places, I enjoyed the company of beautiful women. Many people who had doubts about me quickly became the followers of what they saw the majority pursuing. The minority of people who saw me as a phony became voiceless since the majority no longer accepted anything negative about me.

With time, I became very popular, delivering exactly what they wanted to hear, and that was mendacious promises. When one of the opposition parties began to express its radical views to have all voters pass a basic written or verbal test on the major political issues before being allowed to vote, I strongly criticized them. Since I was a candidate who had emerged from nowhere and quickly risen to fame, they were afraid that a charismatic and ambitious person like myself could influence the minds of ordinary citizens to pay more attention to my promises and forget about the political issues. Honestly, I cared less about people's rights than about doing anything possible to get them to vote for me in the upcoming election. Soon millions of people were fooled into believing that what I was doing was good for humanity, and with this, I became enormously famous. To strengthen my relationship with the poor I fed them empty promises and encouraged them to have faith in the Lord. Becoming wealthy and being constantly showered with praise by people, I was probably the happiest man on Earth. At times I experienced a feeling of guilt in deceiving the poor, but my desire to become rich and famous made me less caring about others.

At the time, the most hotly debated issue of the campaign was same-sex relationships. The pro-active group had grown in size and voice. Realizing that I could gain thousands of votes, I seized the opportunity to become an advocate of same-sex relationships. While my political opponents stressed the importance of moral values, I spoke about people's rights and freedom to choose.

As the date for the national elections grew closer, a survey of the polls indicated that I was the most likely candidate to win the upcoming election. However, during the final week of my campaign, something unbelievably sad happened that seriously affected my career.

It was after visiting a poverty-stricken region that I developed an infectious disease. My entire body became infested with boils, and according to medical reports, they were rare and incurable. Looking at myself in a mirror, I covered my face with both hands and shook my head in disbelief as I could not stand to look at my own disfigured face. I was struck with one of the most horrible diseases a human being could encounter in life.

What was puzzling about this strange disease was that, while my body was totally sore-ridden, I remained in good health otherwise. Due to the severity of it, people avoided contact with me, and consequently, I came to hate everyone. The unpleasant sores all over my body made me despondent. With hardly any friends remaining, and feeling embarrassed by my appearance, I decided to travel to a faraway place to live in hiding.

I became totally dejected and embarked on a lengthy journey by train to the remotest region of the country. Bound for the village of Hadeson, I sat by myself, filled with anger. Being dressed in an outfit which covered most of my body made many people on board eye me suspiciously. Sensing this, I reached into my pocket and took out a blue handkerchief to cover my sore-ridden face, which, however, did not deter people from staring at me.

A young boy who sat on an adjacent seat to me frequently glanced over his shoulder and stared at me. He appeared bored, as he was chewing gum and stretching it in and out of his mouth. His intrusive look greatly annoyed me, so I hastily rose from my seat and approached the lad with my fist clenched tightly to punch him. Instead, I grabbed the boy by his ear and yelled, "Don't you dare look at me again or I will thrash you!" Hearing these insolent words, the frightened lad quietly moved from his seat to another one.

After hearing my angry outburst everyone in the carriage fell silent. It became an uneasy journey for many as they were afraid to talk after seeing the grim look on my face. When the train finally arrived in the village of Hadeson, I stood meditatively and allowed others to get off first since I had no fixed place to go to.

As I stepped off the train, I began reconnoitering the area before deciding where to go. In one particular sector, I noticed a number of small, wooden houses. In spite of them being old and unpainted, I decided to go there in search of a place to rent. Unfortunately, everywhere I went, I was rejected. No one knew anything about me, and they were dubious about trusting me. In these surroundings, I was like a lost sheep in a meadow.

The village of Hadeson was peasant land, rough and isolated. Its population was less than two thousand people, most of whom knew each other well because they worked together daily to plow the small plots of farmland. In this simple, unchanging setting, my presence disturbed the people a great deal. I was a stranger, outlandishly dressed, who seemed to have no visible reasons for being there.

Hadeson was a boring and depressing place. The faces of men and women who lived there were hard and wrinkled from working each day under sweltering conditions. Some people rarely smiled or talked to each other, and I could not tell if my presence triggered changes in their attitudes. In my view, Hadeson was hell on Earth. It was a dreary village, filthy and stinking with old, dilapidated houses separated by a sinuous path of muddy roads. I had never visited a place with so many hard-featured people, who also appeared to be suffering from mental depression.

As I rambled through a narrow track on an open farm lot, I noticed an old, condemned farmhouse on a muddy piece of land. I quickened my pace towards the house and began to knock frantically on the door. I got no answer and, in a fit of anger, I rudely kicked the door open. As I stepped inside the house I was taken aback by the sight of hundreds of cockroaches crawling on the old, wooden floor. Seeing this, I began to grind my teeth in disgust and fury. In a terrible rage, I picked up an old table with broken legs and flung it through the window. I then began to use my heavy boots to crush the scurrying roaches. As I stamped my feet heavily on the floor, the walls of the house vibrated and felt as though they might come crashing down. I was so frustrated that I did not care if the old house did come crashing down on me. Seeing how the floor was becoming soiled by the white, slimy substance that oozed out of the bodies of the roaches, I stopped suddenly. The thought of making this abandoned place my home flashed upon me.

In this rodent-infested farmhouse, I lived alone and in hardship. At night, I slept on fetid haystacks. And with the annoying sounds of bats flying in the dark, it was impossible for me to sleep soundly. I often stuffed pieces of hay into my ears to avoid hearing the early morning sounds of crickets chirping. After a while these tough living conditions became unbearable, and I began to experience the torture of mental suffering. I started terrorizing the local villagers, believing them to be my enemies, and drove fear into the hearts of everyone by threatening to kill them. My profanity kept parents from sending their children out for fear of moral contamination.

The only vestige of joy I got in Hadeson was the familiar sight of people opening their windows and tossing their garbage out. With a scarcity of things to eat, stray dogs would fight over the leftover food. At times I managed a faint smile in the midst of my sorrows, for scantily dressed boys would appear to throw stones at these angry dogs to quiet them.

The people of Hadeson adhered to traditional beliefs, for the elders were highly respected, and their words held authority. After I had been in the village for several weeks, I noticed that a group of elderly men began to assemble each day under a huge tree to perform a series of elaborate rites. They were superstitious and associated all their ill fortune with evil. Watching them from my home, I came to believe that my presence signified something bad, and the elderly men were hoping that this sacrament would bring about change or get rid of me altogether. Annoyed with this, I woke up early one morning and felled the sacred tree with an old axe I had found in the barnyard. From that day on, the men stopped gathering, and I felt relieved by that.

The elders of the village were all scrawny, frail and worn out from hard work and poor nutrition. The women, on the other hand, were more active and seemed in better health than the men. A few days after I had chopped down the tree, some women started to assemble daily in an old two-storied house in the center of the village. Peeking through my window, I began to observe their sneaky activities. It appeared that, whenever I returned home to rest, these women would meet at this particular house to discuss something. After a while, I became suspicious and assumed they were planning to get me out of Hadeson. Believing they were working against me, I decided to put an end to their gossip or whatever plans they had in mind.

A few days later, I stood in front of the two-storied house and began yelling at them to come out. Realizing that they were not responding to my cry, I became enraged and destroyed both the staircases of the house. I felt I had them trapped inside the house. I then began to torment and frighten them by repeatedly throwing stones at the front door. In fear, some of them pushed their heads through a window and began screaming for help. Listening to their cries gave me the feeling that my message was clear—they should never attempt to get rid of me. With no one attempting to help them, I realized their husbands were a bunch of cowards. I was confident now that the village of Hadeson was totally under my control since there was no one to oppose anything I chose to do.

Later, I returned to my old farmhouse to see how these women would get out of the house. Surprisingly, they climbed through an open window and jumped approximately ten feet to the ground to escape. When they did this, I felt disappointed as I was planning to restrict them to the house and torment them each day. However, my disgruntled feelings came to an end when I realized they were no longer a threat to me.

One day, in a violent rage, I began uprooting crops of corn and destroying the homes of my neighbors. It was harvest season and I vividly remember the disconsolate look on people's faces as I destroyed their crops.

After this rampage I stood exhausted amongst the ravaged crops of corn, and slowly a transformation began to take place. I fell to my knees and began to weep. Filled with emotions I cried, "Lord, what wrong have I done that has brought me so much suffering and pain?" I then took the soft mud from the ground and began rubbing it vigorously onto my face. Moments later, I clasped my hands in prayer and took an oath, vowing that, "If I ever found the man who was the cause of all evil things on Earth I would destroy him." After uttering these words I felt a sudden burst of pain in my head and seconds later I felt as though I became separated from my body. I termed the part that was separated from my body, "the true self." From above, I could see my own body lying helplessly on the ground with you, Matthew, standing over me. My true self, which is my thoughts, then began to hover around my body, constantly trying to identify itself with it.

In a buoyant state, I later witnessed some of the villagers moving my body to another location, and wherever they took it, my true self followed closely. As my body was taken away I became deeply saddened sensing that something hurtful had happened to me. I then began to plead with everyone not to take my body away. But my efforts were useless since no one could hear me.

I began to contemplate leaving my body behind and venturing upward into the air. There was, however, something preventing me from doing so. I later discovered that it was because my true self still had a yearning to be with my physical body that made it difficult for me to move upward. Like those who grieve for the loss of a loved one, my true self was grieving for its physical body. After a while, I realized that my body was dead and, when this was clear to me, my true self entered a state of calmness. Subsequently, I felt as though my thoughts were dying, for bit by bit my memories of the past began to fade. Realizing this, I called upon the Lord in prayer not to let me die, but to take me on a journey to learn about life after death. Miraculously, my wish was granted and immediately my true self started moving quickly upward into the air.

On this upward journey, I felt as though I was in my own physical body which I had left behind. As I floated higher, all earthly things began to fade away from my sight. Though I experienced the feeling of still being in a physical body, I was aware that I had left my body behind.

After a while the sky no longer appeared blue. It turned white mysteriously. There was an air of tranquillity and weightlessness. The white surroundings were soon illuminated by an incomprehensible brightness. At this point, the feeling of levitation stopped, and I now felt free to move into places of my own choice. With my true self constantly identifying itself with my body, I still believed that I could act the same as when I had a physical body. In such a frame of mind, I felt as though I could walk, but there was nothing solid below my feet.

As I journeyed through the luminous light, I could not hear the sound of anything or see any form of life. After a while, I became lonely in this infinite region, and in such a melancholy mood, I once again began to think about mundane things. Still concerned about my own physical body, I developed a strong desire to reunite with it. I begged the Lord in prayer to give me back my physical body so that I could search for other forms of life. Again I got what I wished and immediately I began a desperate search for any signs of human life.

After a lengthy journey exploring the region, a man dressed in black appeared out of the radiant light and began walking slowly towards me. In this environment, I felt unthreatened and hurried quickly to meet the strange man. This person looked different from any other human being I had ever seen on Earth. He was very short and old, with piercing red eyes, and carried a staff in his hand.

Realizing that there were no other signs of life, I thought to myself that this man could possibly be God in disguise. Immediately, I began glorifying the name of God and prostrating myself at the man's feet, hoping to be forgiven for all the wrong things I had done on Earth.

The man, totally confused by what I was doing, slowly turned and began to walk away. Still believing that he was God, I began to follow him closely. I continued to glorify the name of the Lord and began pleading with the man to reveal himself. Suddenly, the man stopped and said, "Do not follow me. I am Satan, the devil."

I was taken aback by this shocking declaration, and rudely I said: "Satan, take me to the place where God resides! It is my desire to know the reason for my sufferings on Earth." Satan politely replied, "I know the place where the Lord resides but I am forbidden to enter the kingdom of God or show the way to any sinner." When Satan opened his mouth to speak I noticed that his tongue was black and he had a few teeth missing.

In this unfamiliar region I realized that I could not reach the abode of God without the help of Satan. In an effort to persuade Satan, I encouraged him to join me in seeking forgiveness from God. I tactfully explained to him that the human race held Satan responsible for its own evil doings. They blamed him for being the one who leads them into temptation. I cleverly convinced Satan that God had treated him unfairly, and that he should join me in finding out the reason for our sufferings.

Satan believed that there was an element of truth in what I was saying, and finally he decided to take me to the place where the Lord dwelt. He felt it would be a good opportunity for him to ask God why he was cast into such a lonely place.

On our long journey, I found Satan to be very polite and friendly. Soon we became good friends and enjoyed each other's company. I was very surprised by Satan's courteous behavior; in the past I had always thought of him as being impolite and wicked. However, I was reluctant to trust him, believing that he might yet mislead me.

At last, everything began to get brighter. Believing that we were getting closer to the abode of the Lord, I became doubtful whether God would ever forgive me. Silently in my mind, I began to consider how I could get God to forgive me for my earthly trespasses. I thought to myself that if I killed Satan, then I would be doing the Lord a great favor by freeing the world of all evil. With these thoughts racing through my mind I suddenly pounced upon Satan and began beating him.

Satan was taken by complete surprise, and though repeatedly punched and kicked by me, he did not defend himself. From the many blows to the face, Satan began to bleed profusely. Both his eyes became swollen and practically closed from these heavy punches. I got a feeling of satisfaction from beating the devil because I believed that he was the root of all evil. Tearfully, he pleaded with me not to hurt him. Covering his bloody face with both hands, Satan, in anguish, cried, "Lord, what wrong have I done to deserve such terrible punishments?" I tried every possible way to kill Satan but my efforts were useless since Satan was immortal. I became totally frustrated and angrily walked away from the bloodied Satan.

Everywhere I went, I could hear the crying voice of Satan echoing in the distance. The strange sound not only agitated me but also made me afraid. It was like the eerie sound of a wolf on a dark night. While venturing alone in this unfamiliar region, I realized that it would be impossible for me to find my way without Satan's help. I decided to go back and try to renew my friendship with him.

Upon meeting Satan, I began to resuscitate him. First I apologized, and then cleverly told him that the reason I tried to kill him was to prove that he was indeed immortal. I tried to persuade Satan by telling him that he was someone special whom the Lord uses to test the sincerity and loyalty of mortal beings. This weak attempt to win back Satan's confidence was rejected. A disturbed Satan now spoke with asperity. He said, "You are now my enemy. You cannot be trusted." I was surprised by what I heard. I desperately needed his help to take me to the abode of the Lord. Unable to persuade Satan to join me in my search, I became enraged and began to drag him around by his long, matted hair.

Seeing that Satan was smaller than me, I was confident that I could overpower him anytime. However, when I resorted to profane language, Satan grew furious and, in a fury, picked up his staff and shouted, "I am going to kill you!" It was the first time I had seen Satan in such a terrible rage. In his fury, I noticed that the upper part of his body had begun to transform itself. His neck became longer and his tongue became serpent-like, constantly flicking in and out. His teeth grew longer and protruded outward from his mouth, frothing copiously with saliva from the sides. Satan grew to be eight feet tall with a monstrous face.

I was totally mesmerized by what I saw and stood with my mouth agape in wonder. Aloud, the devil cried: "Know me as the darker side of good for I am pain, suffering and death. I am destruction and all that decays. I am the player in obscenity and infidelity. I am violence, misfortune, darkness and untruth. I am anger, greed and desire. Know me as mockery, intoxication, and all that is iniquitous. No mortal being can destroy me, and I have the power to create evil freely. Only those who choose the path of righteousness can control me. The evils I create enable the human mind to differentiate between right and wrong. Though I reveal myself to you in flesh and blood, know me in truth to be a part of the Infinite One Who is capable of destroying me. To everyone who hates me, let it be known that without my mysterious work, life would be meaningless and unchallenging on Earth."

Hearing these words and seeing the transformation of the devil, I trembled with fear and took to my heels. The moment I started to run, Satan held up his staff and began chasing me. He ran amuck and swung his staff wildly in an attempt to strike me. To avoid being hit I started to run zigzag. During this intense chase, I accidentally stumbled and fell. Seeing this, Satan came charging towards me like a raging bull, but, being too eager to attack, he fumbled with his staff and this allowed me to escape in the nick of time. Within seconds I was back on my feet and running again with Satan close behind.

Totally engrossed with the idea of killing me, Satan paid no attention to the direction in which he was chasing me. It did not occur to him that he was chasing me directly into the abode of the Lord. He suddenly came to a halt when he realized that he was about to enter a forbidden territory.

Angry with himself, Satan threw his staff down and began to stamp his feet. He realized that he could no longer chase after me, and he would have to leave this region. However, before departing, Satan did something unusual. He clasped his hands in prayer and said: "Lord, I am very lonely and I wish to become a mortal being so that I can live a short life like people on Earth. It is my burning desire to know the reason why I am being punished for the evil deeds of others. If I have displeased You in any way, please forgive me, O great Lord."

Bewildered by what had happened, I began to wonder why Satan suddenly stopped chasing me. As I looked back I could see a dejected Satan slowly walking away. At this point, I came to believe that I had finally reached the Lord's abode because I knew Satan was forbidden entry.

CHAPTER 3

In the abode of the Lord, I saw something enigmatic and incomprehensible. The entire place became incredibly bright. Out of the shimmering light, a huge, white, life-like mountain appeared from above and gently lowered itself onto the soft, cushion-like ground in front of me. As I walked cautiously to take a closer look, the intensity of the light lessened. There was no sign of a human-like figure, but I sensed the presence of something with extraordinary power as the huge mountain vibrated fiercely.

I was not afraid of anything because I was determined to confront God to find out the reason for all my afflictions on Earth. Not knowing exactly where to find God, I became incensed and began to condemn and swear at the Lord whom I could not see. Furiously, I cried: "Go down to Earth and see if You can abide by Your own sacred teachings. Those who are caring and compassionate seem to be the ones who suffer the most. I choose to live an unrighteous life because I am able to prosper." In a violent rage I looked in every direction and demanded that God reveal Itself to me.

Suddenly, I began to hear the whooshing of turbulent winds and the crackling noises of thunder. These terrifying sounds were soon followed by a series of extraordinary events. At this point nothing affected me, for I was allowed to witness everything and feel no pain. From these strange happenings, I quickly realized that the Lord was present.

Within minutes the entire mountain became a huge ball of fire that stood aloft. Moments later, I saw this fire put to rest by a torrential downpour of rain that became a deluge. Immediately, an ocean of water with countless fishes and sea creatures appeared, and miraculously everything vanished suddenly.

In its place a vast space of dry land appeared. Once more the rains came and thousands of tiny creatures began to come out of the wet soil. They seemed to have quickened to life as the land became fertile. The majority of them struggled to survive and lived for a very short period. Gradually, these tiny creatures that were produced out of nature itself began to survive longer. Soon they started to multiply and grow in size, and when this happened it appeared to me that their minds were developing too, as the older ones began to foster the new in an effort to secure their survival. In an inconceivable way I was allowed to witness an incredible change in the physical appearance of these beings as they started to become human. Through stages of progressive development I saw how this species, which was only one of its kind, developed both mentally and physically.

In a short time I had witnessed the evolution of a species. This became even more implausible for me because these human beings grew to an average height of seven feet and they looked slightly different in feature from the way I had seen them in earlier stages of development.

Suddenly, the entire place grew dark and the air that they breathed became poisonous. In an instant they all started to die from asphyxiation. It was a horrible sight to see thousands of dead bodies scattered on the ground. Then, as these bodies began to rot, the earth opened up and began to absorb them back into itself.

Once more the land was made fertile and thousands of tiny creatures began to emerge from it, and to me this denoted the beginning of a new cycle. Just as I started to gather some insight about what was revealed, everything vanished from my sight, leaving me totally confused.

After this strange happening, the entire place became populated with rich vegetation and all forms of life. On a small rock, I saw a frog swallowing mosquitoes, then wiggling its way through the tall green grass; a snake appeared and swallowed the frog. Although there were other creatures close to the snake after it had eaten the frog, the serpent did not go on a rampage killing them. The snake only ate what was needed to satisfy its hunger. Observing this, the importance of the law and the order of things dawned upon my mind, for I realized that in order for the serpent to survive it had to abide by the law of the jungle.

Moments later, a raccoon appeared and ate the snake, and as the raccoon lay to sleep, a mosquito appeared and began to suck out its blood. Seeing this, I realized that all creatures are in some way food for one another.

Following that I saw the sun, the earth and the moon merge into one huge planet and from it poured millions of people. I now became an observer to the subsequent events as these people hurriedly became divided into twelve different groups. Just then, the huge planet separated from them and aligned itself to form a parasol over everyone.

Soon, it became alive with action as people from each group began to mingle with one another. Most of them became quarrelsome as their moods grew darker due to conflicting views. Only a small number of people within each group remained composed. Without warning, the next thing I witnessed was the horrifying deaths of millions of these people from various maladies.

When this had ceased, millions of new humans began appearing, but this time there was less confrontation, for in many ways their personalities were unlike those I had seen earlier. Amid the multitude, I saw a group of children who bore a close resemblance to some of the people who had died earlier. Strangely, these children were highly intelligent, for in conversation among themselves, they emphasized the need to create and develop new things of a technological nature so as to make life better. It appeared to me that the true self or thoughts of some of those people who had died earlier from various maladies had somehow taken on the bodies of these children.

After a while everyone vanished leaving me bewildered. With great concern about the meaning of what was revealed, I began to speculate on the things I had seen and what they signified. At first I thought that these twelve groups of people represented the twelve months of the year, during which time the planet would align itself to play a significant role in influencing or shaping the lives of people from the moment they are born.

However, upon reflection of the births of countless human beings with different temperaments, I concluded that after the death of the physical body, one's true self gets refashioned. I believed that there must be some form of silent justice that is served on one's thoughts after death. This justice, I felt, was based upon the merit of one's actions in the previous life and was done with the highest degree of fairness. I also believed that, the universe having billions of people, it was highly possible for people born at different periods of the year to have certain similarities in their personalities, because many had performed virtually the same amount of good or bad actions in their previous life.

In a remarkable show, I witnessed that everything I had seen before begin to merge into one and metamorphose into a massive rock, which quickly changed into a huge ball of fire and then slowly faded away. The entire region became an empty place and I was dazed by this shattering experience. Witnessing this, it dawned upon me that God might be the totality of these objects. I was expecting to see a divine being reveal itself as God, but instead discovered God to be the Universe Itself. These quick changes seemed to have manifested God in different ways. From all that was revealed, it appeared to me that nothing of matter is ever lost as it only changes form and gets absorbed back into nature. I was able to witness the divine power of the Universe and its unending cycle of actions to create, destroy, absorb and recreate things which emanate from Itself.

Still astonished by what had happened, I knelt down and began to pray to God not to show me anything more cataclysmic. However, something even stranger occurred as I suddenly felt separated from my body. I was allowed to witness the most grotesque thing yet, for my body opened up and from it spilled out trillions of living cells. Seconds later, these cells which had formed and supported my physical body started to die rapidly. When they all ceased to exist, my body suddenly closed, leaving me in a state of shock. This made me believe that the true self is the lifeline of all that existed within my body, and it may also be an inconceivable part of God that is the quintessence of life.

Now buoyant, I again saw something incredible, my own physical body gradually aging. Immediately after, I saw myself lying on a bed with my eyes open, and a group of people appeared and took my body away in a coffin for burial.

Moments later, I saw a newborn infant lying on the bed that I had once lain upon. Something unfathomable occurred as my true self entered the body of the infant. From the moment the self came in contact with this new body, sensations began to develop. Soon, the infant began to age, and as it happened, my ideas began to change. Eventually, the infant became a young boy with a violent temper. In this youthful body, I realized that I had a strong desire for earthly things and, as a result, harbored conflicting notions. I began to violently destroy the bed that I had once slept on. After this outrageous act my youthful body suddenly became transformed and I now saw myself as an adult. It seemed as though I had been quickened to life. Though I had momentarily passed through the stages from infancy to adulthood, yet in a mystifying way I was aware of my own actions and the rapid changes.

After analyzing what happened, I became a strong believer in what I termed the "transmigration of refashioned thoughts." I felt that what I had experienced was an indication that I had died, and my true self took on the body of the infant who grew up to be the angry youth. I came to believe that within a few days after death of the physical body all memories of one's past are erased and one's true self enters a state of inactivity until it gets refashioned. It seemed clear to me that, before one's thoughts come in contact with matter, a silent justice is served on the true self. Here, one's thoughts get refashioned according to the merit of his actions. Being refashioned in each cycle of birth and rebirth, the true self is carried from one body to another until it is liberated.

I realized that after conception these refashioned thoughts pick up hereditary characteristics from its parents which assist the mind in its development. Because of the silent justice that is served on the mind these refashioned thoughts need guidance, hence the self amalgamates with the good qualities of its parents. By adopting the qualities of compassion, the physical expression of love, and the instinct of survival, the opportunity for disciplining the mind is provided at an early stage. As a child begins to grow, anger and desire may be two factors of concern. With each person being held accountable for his own actions, the suppressing of anger should be encouraged so that one may become disciplined in speech, mind and conduct.

With a dramatic change of event everything became very dark and I could no longer see anything. In prayer, I cried: "O Lord, do not leave me in this place of darkness but show me Thy light so that I can see Your abode. Please Lord, allow me to live in heaven for one day so that I can know the reward for doing good."

Suddenly, in a spectacular manner, the entire region became wonderfully bright. Once again I felt separated from my physical body, although now I could see my own body lying inert outside the realm of heaven. I realized that this was a sign of my physical body being shed and my thoughts being now my true essence. I quickly experienced a marvelous transformation of myself into something beautiful with a lustrous form. Slowly, I began moving through the air into places of immense beauty. In this state, I felt at ease as my true self was capable of touching things without feeling any form of pain. In this region fear did not dwell.

Soon, I discovered the presence of other beings who were also without a physical shape. These were immortals who had a lustrous and weight-less form. They weren't encased in matter and were free from injury and pain. This radiant form was like the glowing flame of a candle, blissfully floating through the air and only discerned by other immortals.

These immortals had the unique power to transform themselves, and by momentarily allowing themselves to go through the stages of infancy to old age, other immortals were able to recognize them. This provided the opportunity to be reunited with past friends or loved ones in a celestial abode.

I discovered that everyone who dwelled here was at peace with one another and lived in perfect harmony, for harsh words were never spoken. Their heavenly voices which emanated from their radiant form were gentle and pleasing to the ear. I felt uplifted. I realized that my true self was capable of going to wondrous places far beyond anywhere that my physical body could go to. I now enjoyed the feeling of levitation and the freedom to move to places of my own choice.

Here, I saw a variety of plant life all appearing weightless and aglow with rich colors. Flowers were rainbow-hued and appeared lively as they danced placidly through the air, constantly changing shape. Animals and birds which I had seen on Earth were all revealed in shimmering lights which had a form. From the contours of the light which outlined their shape and size, I could tell what creatures they were. Nothing had a physical body and all were blessed with immortality. There was no need for food as nothing revealed was encased in matter. In this region, mountains were weightless and appeared cloud-like and iridescent. Everything that existed dwelled in perfect harmony.

During this wonderful journey, I entered a region where I saw hundreds of species of birds in a lustrous form, whistling enchanting songs as though they were welcoming someone new. As I kept on moving gracefully into this celestial abode, I saw thousands of immortals. From their actions I sensed a oneness in their thinking as they moved forward to welcome me. Together, all the immortals began to change their lustrous forms into individual human embodiments in an effort for me to recognize them. When this happened, I became filled with awe for I saw my beloved parents among the immortals. I became ecstatic and moved swiftly through the air to greet them. We were overwhelmed with joy to see one another. To be reunited with my parents in heaven was the most rewarding moment of my life. In the realm of the immortals, I felt as though I was closely related to everyone, for all that existed dwelt in unity and peace. It was an incredible journey into places of everlasting splendor where my true self never encountered a dull moment.

Unfortunately for me this euphoric feeling suddenly came to an end. Soon, I began to experience the feeling of moving away from this peaceful region to rejoin my physical body. Suddenly, my body was quickened to life, and upon opening my eyes, I discovered myself lying outside the region of heaven. I realized that I was not accepted into heaven for the Lord had only granted me a glimpse of true heaven. As I looked up I saw Satan standing over me, about to strike me with his staff. I cried in anguish: "O Lord, I am a sinner and I have nowhere to go. Please send me back to Earth so that I can serve You, and later gain a place in heaven." The Lord granted me my wish and I felt myself speeding back to Earth. At this point I woke up, just as a huge piece of hardened mud was thrown onto my coffin. I found myself about to be buried.

CHAPTER 4

Recounting his experiences made Dusty feel renewed and charged with energy. He stepped on top of the coffin and quickly hoisted himself out of the hole. Observing that his body was no longer covered in pestilential boils, he felt elated. Dusty Mills began to laugh loudly, thinking that he had fooled the Lord whom he believed had given him a second chance to live. He hurriedly tucked his shirt into his pants and then passed his fingers through his rumpled hair to groom it. His thoughts were now totally fixed on returning to the big city where he could once again enjoy a good life. He walked briskly back to the old farmhouse, where he quickly gathered up his belongings to leave the village and return to his hometown. Meanwhile, Matthew, astonished by Dusty's departure, climbed out of the hole and ran home.

Dusty Mills boarded a train bound for New Hampshire. On this journey, he once again proved that he was capable of influencing people with his ideas. As a "sweet talking" con man, he knew how to act in congenial surroundings with a false face. His charisma was in all its brilliance and, by the time he reached New Hampshire, he had won many new friends. People fell for his charms, and for the old photographs of Dusty in prominent social settings. So great was his ability to allure others that a wealthy couple who was on board the train invited him to their palatial home in a wealthy neighborhood.

Arriving at the house, this elderly gentleman began to gather up the newspaper that was left on the porch. He was shocked to see on the front page a picture of Dusty Mills being wanted for a series of criminal offenses. For a short while, the host remained silent about the matter, allowing his wife to show Dusty their home which was decorated with important and valuable masterpieces. While they chatted, he secretly informed the police of Dusty's whereabouts.

Eventually, Dusty settled in front of the television, anxious to watch the news. He had a strong interest in current affairs, but he was in for a shock. On the screen was his own face. He was the most wanted man in the nation. He made a sudden dash for the door, but was overcome by law enforcement agents who had surrounded the house. Dusty was arrested and had several charges laid against him. It was the most sensational piece of news in a long time. His trial became a media event that was heavily publicized. With the constant media bombardment, the name "Dusty Mills" soon became a household word.

The events surrounding Dusty's court trial were controversial, for it was during his trial that a series of new international laws were put into effect. The new treaty signed by several nations allowed all political leaders to serve only two four-year terms in office. Under the new judicial system a small panel of qualified judges replaced all jurors. And it became a serious offense for politicians to steal or misuse public funds.

What remained puzzling in this case was that, in spite of people learning about Dusty's unlawful practices, they remained loyal and supportive of him. For some unfathomable reason, they refused to view him as a criminal. Dusty Mills began to use religion as a means of gaining public sympathy. He made it known to the news reporters that the Lord had forgiven him for his past wrong doings and had cleansed him of his incurable disease. Many, witnessing that Dusty was no longer infested with boils, believed that he was telling the truth. Dusty's followers believed in his redemption and began to voice their opinion publicly in favor of him. In their view, he was innocent.

When it appeared that justice would not be properly served in this case, those who were swindled by Dusty Mills filed a lawsuit against the government for concealing information about the accused. He was suspected of fraud earlier and not charged, because certain technicalities or flaws in the law prevented Dusty from being apprehended. In a way, the authorities knew about his criminal activities, and by not acting swiftly enough, many more innocent people became his victims.

It was not until the law was challenged that justice was properly served. After a long court hearing, the law found Dusty Mills blameworthy because of the weight of evidence against him. He was sentenced to fifteen years of imprisonment. Due to the nature of the offenses he had committed, he was placed in strict solitary confinement. His only contact with other prisoners was during lunch breaks and exercise periods. Dusty Mills was nonchalant and seemed satisfied in his solitude, since he did not like the idea of sharing his cell with another prisoner. He found prison life quite pleasant as it let him indulge in idleness. He felt that he was better off than the homeless and the deprived, as well as those who lived a lonely life in their homes.

The news on television kept him up-to-date with current affairs. During his lunch breaks he enjoyed playing games with other prisoners, and when alone in his cell, he spent his spare time reading books from the prison library.

These early years of prison life were pleasing to Dusty, but with time the laws changed, and all prisoners had to perform seven hours of compulsory work each day. It became a financial burden for the state to keep people incarcerated for long periods, hence it was mandatory for them to work and learn new skills. At the end of their prison term, they were given a sum of money for all the years they had worked. The money they received gave them the means to merge back into society.

The new system did not suit Dusty. Being now compelled to work seven hours a day greatly disturbed him. He became frustrated, and in desperation he began to pray to God to free him from prison, but this time his prayers were unanswered. Dusty hated the idea of working and this made him disconsolate.

One day while having lunch, he met another prisoner nicknamed Sargon who had become a reformed person. Sargon, seeking atonement for all the wrong things he had done in the past, had become a preacher who was well-versed in the religious scriptures. In time, they became good friends and, on every occasion that they met, the subject of theology was discussed. Sargon strongly believed in God without any rejection of revelation.

Dusty admired the tenacity of his friend in what he believed. However, he had some doubt about many of the things Sargon said as they did not seem rational to him. Sargon was dogmatic in his ideas, while Dusty tried to be more liberal in his views which were largely based on the practical realities of life.

Dusty respected faith and the efficacy of prayer, but he felt that some degree of conjecture or rational thinking must be pursued in order to enrich one's belief and to have a clear understanding of what God encompasses. Some of the things Sargon said greatly influenced Dusty, for he was gradually becoming a reformed person. In spite of being entrenched in his ideas, Sargon was good-hearted, encouraging a confused Dusty Mills to turn a new page in his life.

Over the years, Sargon became very popular with many prison officials as he appeared to be a truly reformed person. Dusty treated him with a great deal of respect. Due to their affinity they trusted each other with many personal secrets. It was from this sharing that Sargon disclosed to Dusty that, although he was seeking to become a reformed person, his real intention was to use preaching as a means of gaining his freedom. From that day on, their friendship dwindled. Dusty realized that he could not trust Sargon.

After many years of living in seclusion, Dusty began to reflect upon what Matthew had told him about being asleep with his eyes open one day and closed the next. He compared this to that moment in his enlightened dream when he felt separated from his body and was able to observe himself lying on the ground. He believed that all those quick changes of events that he had witnessed with his eyes open were related to earthly affairs. Dusty associated the closing of his eyes with death, for he believed that he could not enter the abode of God in a physical body that was subject to pain, disease and death. He compared this experience to that moment when the Lord had granted him his wish to dwell in heaven for a day. He felt that his body had to be cast off to allow his true self to take on a lustrous form. In his view, there was something uncanny about these two events because whatever had taken place seemed to be connected. In analyzing all that had happened, Dusty had mixed feelings about his experience for he believed that it might have been an enlightening dream.

From this memorable experience, Dusty believed that dreams could be of three types. The first is the restless dream in which the mind is in a state of vacillation due to one not being sound asleep. People's thoughts in such restless sleep are usually engrossed with mundane realities.

On the other hand, dreams which occur in deep sleep vary greatly and at times the mind can become deluded, especially if the experience is frightening. While some dreams may be about a pleasant journey in a foreign land, others can go back to early childhood experiences. With dreams that transpire in deep sleep, one not only experiences the false feelings of actually tasting, touching and seeing things, but also those of movement, fear and pain.

Dusty believed that in the third type of dream, seemingly in "dream-less" sleep, the experience is one of tranquillity which differs tremendously from a dream in deep sleep. In such a peaceful dream of dwelling in emptiness there is nothing to hear or to be afraid of. In a dreamless sleep, the feeling of being in a physical body is practically lost and the mind does not desire anything. He felt that upon awaking from such a dreamless sleep, one can only reflect upon a slight awareness of dwelling in calmness.

In analyzing these various types of dreams and comparing them with his past experiences, Dusty realized that there was a broader meaning to his dreams. He strongly believed that the true self of a person is his thoughts, which are constantly refreshed by the ongoing activity of thinking or dreaming. In dreams, the mind remains active to prevent one from becoming dysfunctional. Even in a dreamless sleep one is aware of what such a dream is like, sensing afterwards that it is something tranquil.

Reflecting upon his past experiences when he had fallen into a coma, he realized that, in spite of being unconscious, his mind had remained active. With a passionate desire to know the reason for his sufferings, his thoughts journeyed into the unknown in search of the answer. Those random thoughts which made him aware of things during the day were similar to those which made him aware of his own existence when asleep. He believed that as long as he was alive his thoughts remained with him. It was the extraordinary rate at which his thoughts varied that made it difficult to remember all his dreams and experiences. Dusty remained puzzled as to whether his heavenly experience was a dream or whether God had truly revealed something divine to him.

CHAPTER 5

After ten years of incarceration, Dusty Mills was allowed to leave twice a week on parole. He received a portion of his own money that had been saved by the government for all the years he had worked in prison. He badly needed new clothes and was eager to go shopping since he did not want to be seen in public wearing the old prison attire.

As he walked along a narrow cobblestone street in a busy shopping area, he was approached by a gang of men who, for unknown reasons, began to tease him. This sudden confrontation grew into an altercation, which in a short time broke out into a vicious fight. Dusty was badly beaten by the gang and robbed of his money. As he sat on the ground, his nose bleeding, the thought of being a victim dawned upon him as he finally realized how others felt being robbed. At this point, he felt that life was a chance to ameliorate oneself and he had missed that opportunity.

A woman witnessing the incident hurriedly came to assist him. At her sudden appearance, the gang quickly dispersed and vanished. The woman compassionately helped him to his feet. She waited for him to regain his composure and then introduced herself as Samantha Moore. Thinking that Dusty was probably a homeless man, Samantha offered to buy him something to eat. Dusty accepted her invitation with alacrity and together they went to a nearby café, where he told her that he was a prisoner, out on parole.

At first she was reluctant to keep his company, but Dusty being a "sweet talking man" convinced her that he was someone whom she could trust. He encouraged her to meet him often at the café. Surprisingly, she accepted his invitation. Their meetings, which had begun purely innocently, soon grew into a love relationship.

Samantha was a wealthy and educated woman. She loved fashionable clothes and made the most of life by enjoying whatever it had to offer. Her snug clothes on a shapely body were impeccable, showing her to be a sophisticated lady. Between her full lips, her white teeth sparkled which made her smile all the more alluring. In short, she was gorgeous. She was the most beautiful woman Dusty had ever seen and he adored her. With friends, Samantha was a jovial person who enjoyed making others laugh. But in her social life she showed balanced judgment by being methodical and dignified in her actions.

After meeting with her on several occasions, Dusty discovered that she was an atheist. Whenever his favorite subject of religion was discussed, Samantha would remain uninvolved. What remained puzzling to Dusty was that, despite being a non-believer, she was a compassionate and generous person, especially to the needy.

After months of getting to know each other, they agreed to get married, and Dusty anxiously applied to the government to grant him permission to marry Samantha. Many of the inmates doubted that the authorities would accept his application, but Dusty later surprised everyone when he received this approbation. Being up-to-date with current affairs, he was much better informed than the other prisoners, and he had even taken time to learn about recent changes in the law.

Dusty loved his wife and, while on parole, he made every possible effort to be with her. She meant a great deal to him and he treated her with respect. After two years of marriage, Samantha gave birth to a boy, and Dusty was overjoyed. The newborn infant soon brought about significant changes in Samantha's personality. Her desires changed as certain things that once gave her personal joy became less important. She now began to spend most of her time taking care of the young child and performing her duties as a responsible parent.

Dusty's son grew up to be a polite and well-mannered boy who loved his parents. He wanted to be with his father daily, but this was impossible because Dusty still had to finish the remaining part of his prison term. Dusty became closely attached to his family and felt that, while friends come and go, his family was here to stay. He promised his son that after he was released from prison, he would spend more time with him. Such an optimistic promise, however, never came to fruition.

It was while sitting quietly in prison one day that he received the shocking news that his wife and son had been killed in a car accident. This news was heartbreaking because they were the source of all his joys. In a confused frame of mind, Dusty turned violent and began kicking the prison walls, swearing and fighting with the prison guards. He demanded that he be released immediately so that he could be with his family. His behavior was totally unacceptable to the authorities, and this resulted in him being forbidden to see his family or to attend their funeral.

The tragic news of their untimely death shattered Dusty completely. It caused him unbearable grief, and he lamented each day. Dusty could not accept the death of his son, and in anguish he prayed to God to bring his son back to life. The love for his wife and son was so strong that he grieved each day for the remainder of his prison term.

After many sad years in seclusion, Dusty Mills was finally released. With the final installment of his earnings, he rented a small one-bedroom apartment on the outskirts of the city. The years had aged him considerably and he felt lonely living by himself. In a desperate attempt to win new friends, he tried showing his neighbors old photographs of himself in the company of many famous people. From the half-hearted response he got, he soon realized that no one really cared.

The attitudes and lifestyles of people had changed considerably over the last fifteen years while he was in prison. In order for him to maintain stability of mind, he realized that, as he got older, he had no choice but to start adapting to a more liberal society.

The man who was once known for his good looks now realized that he was entering the final phase of his life. He looked grey and wrinkled. Although he was now a free man, he felt like a prisoner trapped within the four grey walls of his apartment. Thinking that he might not live much longer, the thought of equality dawned upon him. He finally realized that he was not superior to anyone since death happens to all.

On several occasions he visited a private investigation agency to find out what was the real cause of the fatal accident in which his family was killed. It was during one of these visits that he learned something new. A police officer who was at the scene of the accident reported that, as his wife lay on the ground drenched in blood, she repeatedly said under unbearable pain, "O Lord, please help me!"

Dusty knew that his wife was an atheist, but hearing that she had uttered those words, he concluded that there are certain intrinsic thoughts about God which reside within all human beings. He believed that in some people these thoughts are suppressed, as the mind may be too occupied with earthly desires, and in times of adversity or with the coming of old age, one's inner feelings may be silently or verbally expressed.

With time, Dusty gradually began to accept the death of his family. Unable to cope with the stress of loneliness, he decided to travel to a special region of the country named Gillsburg to do penance.

CHAPTER 6

The county of Gillsburg comprised a few small villages which were mainly inhabited by pilgrims, and fishermen and their families. This region was known for its serenity, lush plants and exotic flowers. Many came here to seek knowledge about God through meditation.

Dusty chose to live in a small village called Sutton which was peaceful and sparsely populated. His favorite place to relax was under the shady trees along the banks of the river. He believed that by coming here to do penance, God would one day allow him to be reunited with his family.

After months of living among wise men, Dusty gathered a great deal of spiritual knowledge from them. Their words of wisdom were comforting to him and gradually he began to gather inner strength to alleviate his sorrows.

One day, on his journey to a local shrine, he saw a middle-aged man sitting under a shady tree, meditating. The man's appearance was different from the other sages as he was neatly dressed and his face cleanly shaven. Slowly, he approached the man and, in an act of humility, prostrated himself at his feet. Still saddened by the loss of his loved ones, he wanted to tell the man the tragic story of his family.

The man slowly opened his eyes and began to look at him curiously as if they had met before. He gave a delighted smile and then uttered the name, "Dusty Mills!" He greeted Dusty with an affectionate pat on the shoulder and introduced himself as Matthew. Hearing that name, Dusty quickly realized that he was the young boy, Matthew, who had grown to an adult. They were delighted to meet each other and, both having an interest in meditation, soon became companions in the spiritual quest for knowledge.

Dusty was eager to hear from Matthew the reason for his coming to this sacred place. He was surprised to learn that it was because of a promise Matthew had made to honor the Lord. Matthew told Dusty that, while he lay in the coffin to be buried, Matthew had taken a solemn oath that if Dusty were brought back to life, he would serve God forever. Dusty was deeply touched, for he remembered his enlightened dreams and the broken promises he had made to serve the Lord.

Becoming emotional, he took a vow that he would never hurt anyone and would turn over a new leaf to follow the path of righteousness. Matthew was sympathetic and trusted him to become a truly reformed person. As they exchanged ideas, both of them became knowledgeable in theology and developed a common objective of gaining knowledge about God.

Dusty, by devoting time to the contemplation of God, soon began to think less about his deceased family. He came to conclude that all who are born must die and all who have not been liberated must be reborn in a new human body. The wise men were delighted to see that he had begun to find peace within himself.

Early one morning, while sitting under a shady tree close to the river, Dusty noticed a short, elderly man walking slowly towards him. As the man got closer, he felt uneasy. His face suddenly became reddened with anger and took on a menacing look. With his fist tightly clenched he stared at the man and yelled, "You are Satan! What are you doing here?" In reply the man humbly said, "I am not Satan, I am a pilgrim. I came here because I was invited by the sages to give a sermon on how to control one's anger."

It appeared that the pilgrim resembled the short, old Satan figure whom Dusty had seen in his enlightened dream while unconscious. Seeing him, Dusty became angry and confused. He felt convinced that Satan, the devil, had come to Earth. His mind became filled with conflicting thoughts as he relived that moment in his dream when he was beating Satan.

Turning violent, Dusty began to beat the innocent man. He accused him of causing the death of his wife and son. This harmless man was beaten and choked to death by Dusty who was overjoyed by what he had done, thinking that he had freed the world of all evil. Immediately, he ran to call the sages to look at the dead man whom he called Satan.

The sages were taken aback by what they saw. The man he killed was indeed someone special whom they had invited. The sages hurriedly gathered around the dead man and decided to take the body away to another location. Dusty tried to convince them that the man was indeed Satan for he had met him in the past. The wise men shook their heads in disbelief and remained silent.

Matthew was in a state of shock by Dusty's violence and seemed bewildered by this careless act. He felt betrayed because of the promise Dusty had made to live a righteous life. While he continued throughout his life to have confidence in others, he never again trusted anyone completely, feeling that he could no longer rely on the integrity of another person.

Worried, Dusty Mills walked slowly over to Matthew and asked in a humble voice, "Is this man whom I have killed really a spiritual leader?" Matthew nodded his head, and Dusty turned and began to walk towards the river. Matthew sensed that he was going to commit suicide, so he followed him closely. He pleaded with him not to go into the river as it was infested with flesh-eating crocodiles. Distraught, Dusty Mills completely ignored him and walked into the river. Desperately trying to keep his head above the water, he cried out to Matthew: "I am food for these hungry creatures and they in turn are food for another. Know

God as the universe in its entirety. My thoughts are my true self and in a few days all my memories of the past will be erased. My mind will enter a state of dormancy and then be refashioned according to the merit of my actions."

Slowly, the hungry crocodiles began to surround him. Using their powerful jaws, they viciously attacked his legs, ripping apart his flesh. He offered no resistance but simply allowed himself to be eaten. In a last and desperate attempt, Dusty managed to get his head above the water, but this time he said, "Forgive me, O Lord, for in my heart I know that I was unfaithful to Thee, but please, in my next life give me a new body so that I can better serve Thee."

Finally, there were no more signs of Dusty, except for some torn pieces of clothing which floated up to the top of the water. Matthew slowly turned and walked away. He realized that Dusty Mills was confused by his own blunder and his undisciplined mind had caused him great suffering. However, the words that he uttered moments before he died later conveyed significant meaning to Matthew in his own quest for spiritual knowledge.

CHAPTER 7

Through the years, Matthew lived a quiet life in the company of wise men. He frequently thought about Dusty Mills, who had died a very confused man. The things he said and believed in caused Matthew to ponder. It appeared to him that Dusty had some knowledge about God, but had failed to discipline himself judiciously in following the righteous path. He felt that Dusty's fickle mind was the major cause of most of his earthly sufferings.

Having lived among sages for many years, Matthew realized that their lives were free of earthly desires since they seemed pleased and content with life. He was frequently told by them of an inner peace and also the feeling of being liberated that they found during meditation.

Matthew, however, was not completely satisfied with the idea of being liberated, for he wanted to have a clearer understanding about God and life after death. He believed that anyone who lived a righteous life and sought knowledge about God by reasoning with oneself could become a seer who could share words of wisdom with others.

Reflecting upon some of the things Dusty had said, he believed that, even though he had been a confused man, what he had said seemed to reflect a deeper meaning of God. In seeking to understand what other sages were experiencing in meditation, he decided to try their method in the hope of experiencing the feeling of liberation that they described.

One day, while meditating, he fell into a dreamlike state in which there was practically nothing to think about. He was fully reposed, and in such a frame of mind, he could not remember what it was that he had set out to achieve. He felt surrounded by emptiness with practically all senses lost. It was a peaceful experience with a slight awareness of dwelling in an empty space and not being confined by anything.

After he came out of this dreamlike state, he began to analyze what he had experienced. He felt a little disappointed as he was unable to gain any clear form of knowledge about God. Matthew strongly believed that this experience was a false idea of freedom. In reality, he had gone nowhere.

In the weeks to follow, he became less interested in this form of contemplation. He believed that there must be other ways of acquiring knowledge about God. He felt that the lives of these sages were restricted and lacked challenges. Their sedentary life was not to his liking; the idea of spending a lifetime sitting and meditating was not quite conducive to his way of thinking. He believed that those who performed selfless and righteous actions were equal in their efforts to those who only practiced meditation, since both are capable of freeing themselves from the cycle of birth and rebirth. He greatly admired their tenacity in seeking a way to everlasting freedom, but he also believed that people could perform their civic duty and acts of benevolence, and thus still achieve liberation.

On a warm, sunny day, as he leisurely walked along the banks of a river, he saw a group of sages talking to a woman who held a young child in her arms. Their conversation was a lengthy one, and suspecting that it might be important, he decided to inquire. He soon learned that the woman was a widow who had brought her disabled daughter to the shrine in hope that the sages would help to foster the young girl. The widow claimed that she was too poor to raise her child. She felt that by coming to this place to seek help, these holy men might show some compassion for her disabled daughter and assist her. However, the answer she got from the sages surprised her for they declined to help her, claiming that the child would greatly hinder them in their spiritual quest.

The widow was disheartened by the sages' refusal to help her child. Unable to cope with rejection, she became angry and began to criticize them for their egocentricity. In a strong voice she yelled at the holy men not to preach to others about love for humanity since they did not practice what they sermonized.

Matthew, realizing that there was an element of truth in what the widow was saying, quickly intervened to mollify her. He felt betrayed and saw this episode as an example of selfishness shown by holy men. He was disappointed, knowing that these sages glorified the name of God daily, and yet they would not take part in the pious act of helping another in a time of distress.

As the widow was about to leave, Matthew approached her and said: "I will assist you in fostering your child and you can forever trust me to never want to abandon her. I will raise her like a daughter and ensure that she is provided with the necessities of life." The young girl, whose name was Rebecca, was extremely pretty but she was paralyzed from the waist down. On the mother's face he saw signs of grief, but on that of the young girl there was a pleasant smile. The widow was in her mid-thirties with tangled hair that seemed unwashed. She looked fatigued and pitiful. It was easy to tell that she dwelled in poverty, for her long fingernails were filled with dirt from scavenging people's garbage.

Soon life became full of meaning for Matthew as he gave up contemplating God and began providing for the young child. Every day, he journeyed to Rebecca's home taking food and, at times, new clothing. He showered the young girl with affection and kindness, and brought joy into her life. After some time, she became very attached to him, believing that he was her father. Each day she would sit by her window and wait patiently for him to arrive. Together, they were like a family, except that Matthew did not live at their house. As time passed, these daily visits became troubling to Rebecca because she could not grasp the reason for his departures. As she got older she confronted Matthew more frequently about his leaving. Why he could not live with them was her incessant question.

Matthew feared to answer, thinking that he might hurt her feelings. He was not ready to disclose that he was not her real father and, besides, he had no desire to be the target of gossip. This was perhaps the only flaw in what was otherwise a perfect relationship.

After devoting many years to the care of Rebecca, Matthew realized that he was getting older, and his desire to know God was getting stronger. It was in this final phase of his life that he became much more resolute to gain knowledge about God. Over the years, he had heard from other sages about a new method of acquiring spiritual knowledge called "conscientious contemplation." He had heard that it was an inspiring and rational approach to gaining knowledge. Being unsuccessful with other forms of contemplation, he was eager to try this new method. It was taught at a place nine miles from his home.

He realized that to leave this town to learn something new meant he would have to make a critical decision about separating himself from Rebecca and her mother. It was a tense and emotional period for Matthew. After a long deliberation, he decided to disclose his intentions of leaving. The widow's reactions were most uncharacteristic. She insulted him so harshly that Matthew felt his credibility was at stake. He was accused of breaking his solemn promise. So enraged was the widow that the veins on her forehead swelled and her face reddened with anger. Filled with contempt, she roughly picked up her daughter and angrily walked away. Matthew felt ashamed and utterly dejected. The bitter words continued to ring in his ears. He bowed his head and quietly walked away, deeply disturbed by the widow's cruel denouncement.

The accusations demoralized Matthew because he realized that he too had breached the trust of another person. He reflected upon Dusty's broken promises of never wanting to hurt anyone. He realized that he too had failed, but at the same time, he felt that it was not fair of others to fully rely on his integrity.

Matthew's decision to leave greatly angered many as there was much sympathy for the disabled child. He was severely criticized, but in spite of this he remained steadfast in his resolution to learn about conscientious contemplation. He felt that he had been too harshly judged. His one selfish act had made him an outcast and a sinner, he thought, whereas Dusty's heinous acts had gone virtually unpunished. Matthew began to think that perhaps his timidity had made him an easy target while Dusty's violent temper had shielded him from criticism. He reasoned that no one criticized Dusty because they were afraid of him.

As Matthew pondered further, he realized that he too had never voiced his opinion in opposition to Dusty's criminality. This led him to believe that there was a form of weakness on the part of himself and others which caused them to succumb to the aggressor. He realized that if unrighteous acts were not opposed by anyone then the unrighteous would rule the Earth.

Matthew felt that those who are very educated or caring, and show empathy or compassion towards others, often tend to become faint-hearted. It appeared to him that what might be considered good or bad stems from a Single Source, with both being controlled by that very Source. During the course of his life, he witnessed the gradual process of rejuvenation and rebuilding from destruction. Many of the things he considered bad, such as acts of destruction by nature, human atrocities and even the criminal acts of Dusty Mills, seemed to reflect some of the sorrowful experiences in life from which a valuable lesson could be learnt. Dusty's sinful acts taught him to stay clear of all reprehensible motives and desires. He came to believe that one's duty or moral obligation to uphold law and righteousness should be remembered even when the transgressor is one's own kin or friend. He concluded that, in order to maintain fairness, unity and peace on Earth, the strength of statutory laws was a crucial factor in determining how evil is suppressed and unity sustained.

Once in the new village, he was eager to learn the method of gaining spiritual knowledge. He learned that the form of meditation these sages practiced was quite different from his. It was a new and rational approach which involved a mental journey into one's thoughts.

They began their quest for knowledge by first selecting questions of their own choice regarding God and the universe, and then silently in their minds they would begin to speculate on them, hoping to find the answer. This method of contemplation was practiced prior to bedtime or sitting in a quiet place during the day.

It took Matthew nine nights of contemplation to gain the answers to these nine questions.

Does God exist?

What is God?

Why should I believe in God?

What is the purpose of life?

What things give form to life?

What is my true self?

Is there life after death?

How can I heal my undisciplined mind?

What is the reward for doing good?

As Matthew lay in bed one night, he closed his eyes and began a mental journey into his thoughts. He focused his thoughts on the question "Does God exist?" and allowed this subject to dominate his mind. After an intense period of speculation, he could not find anything substantial that could prove the existence of God.

Matthew realized that from early childhood he had been brought up in a home where religious sentiments had not been instilled in him. Reflecting back upon the time when Dusty was about to be buried, he realized with unbearable guilt that something had made him instinctively call upon God to bring Dusty back to life. He realized that the question of whether or not God exists lies in one's own personal belief.

It was while speculating on the subject of life after death and searching mentally for ways to explain the phenomena of nature that he finally accepted the notion that God exists. He then proceeded to speculate on the purpose of the universe with such a diverse display of things which he could see with his naked eyes.

By reasoning with himself, he slowly realized that, if the universe were left in darkness, empty and with no form of life, then it would certainly be useless as there would be nothing to see. He concluded that there must be something of extraordinary power that reveals itself in great diversity, and therefore, that which exists certainly leaves room for appreciation and belief. He felt convinced that everything revealed stemmed from a single source.

With further speculation, he realized that everything which emanates from that source must be maintained, and only something infinite is capable of doing so. This led him to conclude that God is the Universe Itself. When he reached this point of speculation, the answers to his questions began to unfold.

The knowledge Matthew acquired in conscientious contemplation was not a divine revelation. Instead, he achieved spiritual knowledge by reasoning with himself. The essence of his beliefs is unveiled in the following message.

*   *   *

In contemplation it dawned upon him that God may be the Universe in its entirety and this Single Source of everything could be ubiquitous. He viewed this Divine One to be revealed in the infinite diversity of things which are both animate and inanimate. And that everything seen with the naked eye is only an infinitesimal part of It. Even though he thought of God as amorphous, he believed the Lord to have semblance.

From conjecture, he came to believe that matter is eternal, and everything that we breathe, touch, taste and see emerges from a single source called God. He felt that the Divine Lord is infinite, birthless and everlasting.

He thought that in order for God to maintain everything which emanates from Itself, this Source in an extraordinary way has to perform perpetually even to sustain its own Self. He felt that everything which is revealed by God has a special purpose in its own unique way. And regardless of how we view its functionality, it remains an integral part of that which maintains the equilibrium of things.

Matthew perceived creation as an epiphany of God, and felt that everything revealed will slowly change its form with time. To him, all human beings emanated from God and were in a constant cycle of birth and rebirth. Through contemplation, he came to believe that the abode of the Almighty One is everywhere and is not confined by space. He thought that from this Single Source whence we emerge, all beings are possibly set in motion to maintain the harmony and the equilibrium of things.

Matthew believed that, to remain in unity with the Source, he needed to perform his civic duties and acts of benevolence. He feared that, if driven by various forms of desire, he could become lost in greed and drift away from the Source. He perceived that while many sought to destroy their own kind or other forms of life, God at times worked in unexpected ways to prevent this from happening. With a belief that the universe is revealed in infinite diversity, he felt that such variety made life interesting for human beings to explore, discover and learn things.

Matthew felt that believing in God was a way of identifying himself with the Divine Source, so that it would help to strengthen his moral obligations. For in so doing, there is a calling for him to perform acts of goodness. In his view, knowledge about God would help him to live in unity with the Source and nature.

It dawned upon him that in times of adversity there was a tendency for a dying person to think about God, loved ones, or life after death. He felt that the fear of his own death, and the quest to explain the phenomena of nature, were two factors that encouraged him to believe in God. In considering God to be the Universe in its entirety, he felt that seeing what was revealed by the Lord was a reality for him. Within this, he visualized everything that surrounded him—the sun, the ocean, and all forms of life—to be part of God. And with a belief that God revealed Itself in diversity, he felt convinced that he could actually see a part of God in which he himself was a very minute part.

Matthew came to believe that God sustained all life in a way that is inconceivable until the death of their physical bodies. He believed that after death, if his true self was not liberated, it would shortly thereafter enter a state of dormancy and all of his memories of the past would be erased. Such memories were erased so as to prevent chaos and blame for one's wrong doings in a past life. This, he felt, was not the demise of one's thoughts, because one's true self may get refashioned and enter a new body to continue in another cycle.

He realized that, for the true self to enter a state of tranquillity, it should relinquish its earthly desires, or else it would remain a wandering force. Through the transmigration of refashioned thoughts one's true self moved from one body to another until it healed itself, and when in contact with a new body, the true self would most likely pick up hereditary characteristics which would help the mind in its development. In his view, when refashioned thoughts or the true self came in contact with the matter of a new human body, sensations were created. He believed that the mind will mature with time but the bodies of all beings will in the end cease to exist.

A mind not healed in one life had the chance of healing itself in another. This thought comforted him, because in this light even the unrighteous had scope for betterment. Matthew felt that, while he might not be perfect in all his actions, yet in striving for perfection he could become liberated. It was useless for him to spend a lifetime performing unrighteous acts and expect to be pardoned by God in the final moment of his life. He believed that his true self was his thoughts, and once liberated, nothing could affect it.

In Matthew's view, one's thoughts were not matter but were encased in matter; the way they function may vary, especially if the brain is affected by disease or severe injury. While many believe that one's thoughts immediately die at death, Matthew felt that one had to delve into the mystery of thought itself. One's thoughts, he believed, were the true self of a person, and after death it only enters a restful state or functions in a way that is not understood by us.

Matthew, in searching for a reason to believe in God, felt that it would be totally useless for the Infinite One to leave the universe in darkness, empty and with no form of life. But to allow an infinite variety of things to emerge from Itself creates the possibility of believing in a Divine One. He believed that which emerges from God should be maintained, and pure actions help to do that. It is difficult for unrighteous acts to maintain anything, for such ungodly actions in the end lead to chaos or moral degradation.

In contemplation it dawned upon him that the purpose of life was to maintain the harmony of things by performing those actions that would lend continuity to life and the amelioration of all. Hence, there must be unity, compassion and the desire to share the simple joys of life which bring comfort and happiness to others. He felt that while life should be enjoyed in a way that pleases the mind, a certain dignity and respect should be maintained in one's deportment. He saw that, as the mind matures, human beings realize how their desires change as the factors of old age, sickness and loneliness become a growing concern.

Matthew believed that what emanates from God is an external view of an infinite number of things which human beings can see with their naked eyes. He felt that, in a physical body, humankind has the opportunity to witness what is revealed and to play a vital part in sustaining the harmony of things.

Upon reflection of his life experiences, Matthew came to the conclusion that, for him to discover something graceful and distinctly new, he would have to dwell within or take refuge in that Infinite One. The experience in the inner realm of God is one without the body, and here, the liberated mind finds everlasting peace and bliss.

Life is comprised of two separate orders of experiences: the first within the physical body, the second, without. The former, he believed, was a mixture of both joy and sorrow. Within his physical form he can experience grief and pain. The separation from one's loved ones is a form of suffering, and it is the close attachment to loved ones that causes him grief. With the physical body people procreate and, in family life, share the feelings of love with their offspring. In intimate relations there is continuity and genetic heredity. The other experience is outside the physical body and occurs after death. Here, the liberated self takes on a lustrous form, and in this radiance, the true self is free of pain and desire. Freed from all constraints and limitations, it remains imperishable.

Matthew concluded that evil is unrighteous thoughts which could make him perform sinful acts. Anger and evil desires ought to be suppressed to discipline his mind. He believed that he is held accountable for his own actions, and another should not be blamed for his wrong doings. He felt that, if driven by various forms of desire, he may fail to identify with the Source, thus he may become a follower of unrighteousness. To him, evil desires deprive one from becoming liberated, and the Divine One takes no part in one's good or bad actions.

In Matthew's view, the cycle of creation and destruction brought forth diversity. Just as an old crumbling building is resurrected with a new appearance, so too is one generation replaced by another with different characteristics. To him, existence was a cyclical and unbroken chain as long as one's true self was not liberated. He believed that the longer his mind took to heal itself, the longer he would remain in the cycle of birth and rebirth.

He realized that, while many seek spiritual knowledge to gain liberation, others struggle in their own efforts to serve humanity. Those who believe in fairness, and work diligently to maintain the law and to ensure that justice is properly served, are in a way performing acts of goodness.

He thought about how many contribute to the preservation of things by seeking to find a cure for human illnesses. He felt that the efforts of these people should be appreciated even if they do not always bear fruit. Also, many do not seek spiritual knowledge but dwell among the poor and the deprived, seeking to help and comfort them. He believed that such responsible acts could liberate the self, since such people practiced modesty, love and compassion to live in unity with God.

Matthew felt that the evil acts committed against the innocent should be opposed, and he should be outspoken against injustice. He believed that, by people remaining nonchalant about injustice, evil is propagated, and for him to remain silent means that in a way he is silently collaborating with evil. Matthew thought about those who support the leadership of a tyrant out of fear, and those who become the victims of such an evil person. He felt that those who know in their hearts that such acts are ungodly but continue to support such an oppressor are deluded.

In contemplation about the law, he felt that those who perform ungodly acts and are set free by technicalities in the law only mislead themselves into believing they are exonerated. In his view, no mortal being can escape the silent justice of God that is served on one's thoughts, because it is the only one that is wholly fair and faultless. He believed that this silent justice is not served on the physical body, but determines the way one's thoughts get refashioned, causing each person to be born with a different temperament. How disciplined he was in action, speech and conduct helped him to assess the level of his own sufferings.

Matthew felt that law and education are two factors which help to prevent crime, and when the law is too lenient crime proliferates. He felt that flawed and poor laws were useless if they failed to bring about justice. Laws must be fair and purposeful, and upheld to prevent chaos. They should be enforced to prevent the innocent from suffering. Those who believe in fairness and strive to keep up the harmony of things are in a way bringing themselves closer to liberation. The laws that are created by human beings to maintain order and fairness will never be perfect in their entirety, as many wrong doers are never brought to justice. However, with the silent justice of the Lord, even one's most secret or devious act gets judged, and one's thoughts are refashioned in accordance with the merit of one's actions.

On the subject of diversity, Matthew felt that, though all beings emanate from the same Source, there is a tendency for most of them to want to be with their own kind. Such beings, in wanting to protect, will oppose others if harm is done to their own or if their survival is threatened. He believed that, when human beings fail to appreciate and understand what is revealed in the great diversity, racist sentiments take hold. These prejudiced feelings seem to stem from an intrinsic quality which is linked to the human instinct to survive. They appear to lie dormant in early childhood and slowly grow as the mind encounters difficult challenges in life which may include anger, discontent or hurtful experiences. When one dislikes the physical characteristics or beliefs of others, hatred forms in the deluded mind, thus threatening unity.

He felt that many deceive others by feigning unbiased feelings; however, a liberated mind has no biased feelings for it is thoughtful and benevolent. And in unity with nature such a disciplined mind sees equality in all. Humankind, through various forms of knowledge, plays a vital role in maintaining the harmony and the equilibrium of things. Through its efforts to uphold order and to help others, it is to some degree one part of God assisting another part to sustain itself. Matthew thought that many who are fascinated by medical achievements which improve the quality of life may become doubtful about the existence of God. Such people are unaware that the humane acts of those who help others are a part of God, and they may need to reflect on how the Lord works mysteriously at times through the efforts of a learned one to ease the suffering and pain of others.

Concerning the horrific acts of nature and other calamities, he thought that many fear the coming of a cataclysmic end in which everything will be dissolved. Matthew believed that, to ensure there is continuity of life, God the Preserver works mysteriously through human efforts and nature to sustain things. Despite his belief that God is the Universe in its entirety, this did not mean that one should worship every aspect of nature. He believed that through the path of spiritual knowledge human beings may have a better understanding of what God encompasses.

Matthew felt that there was no need for him to perform excessive sacrifices or penance to gain spiritual liberation. In his view, following the right path would put an end to the cycle of birth and rebirth. He believed that there were many paths to one God, and whatever path one chose, it should constitute acts which are righteous. Because people are at different stages of spiritual development, he believed in religious respect and tolerance. It struck him that the wonderful things people had built to assist themselves in identifying with God helped to shape their lives. Prayer itself, he felt, is one way of identifying ourselves with God and motivating us to do good. Matthew respected those who perform the short and purposeful rituals of worship since it gives meaning to their lives.

Matthew felt that, in atonement for one's sins, an effort should be made to avoid performing ungodly acts. Through the performance of acts of goodness, anyone in this present cycle could liberate themselves from the cycle of birth and rebirth.

Human behavior could be divided into three types: the wicked, the average, and the righteous. Evil doers are angry and violent, lawless and lazy. Such people rarely reflect upon their actions, hence they may remain in the dark or in trouble with the law. He concluded that the degree of their torment was in direct proportion to the merit of their actions in their previous life. However, in spite of their unethical behavior, they were free to alter their own temperament, as the qualities of the mind are not fixed. He believed that through the path of knowledge they could change themselves into righteous or lucid people.

The average are those who vacillate between good and bad deeds, and are usually indecisive about what path to follow. Such people are confused by their own desires, and in this state of vacillation their minds become deluded. This group is likely to be moody and easily agitated, and are driven by a desire to acquire things of material value. Despite their confusion, however, they play a vital role in furthering the economic growth of society with many of their good deeds. And due to some of their good efforts, they are silently rewarded as their suffering is far less than those who may be fully evil.

The righteous are the caring, compassionate, calm and contented lot. They had performed many pious acts in their previous life and are here to bring themselves closer to liberation. He felt that this group was non-violent, modest, truthful and does not crave for reward. They realize that true happiness cannot be found in a physical body which is subject to pain and death.

In meditating upon life after death, it dawned upon him that a true heaven is that special place where the liberated self dwells in peace, bliss and perfect harmony with everything. Here, he believed, the true self is not encased in matter or confined by anything. And in a lustrous form it dwells in places of immense beauty. He believed that in the company of other liberated beings there is unity and peace, as the true self is free of anger and desire.

Matthew believed that, in a celestial abode, the true self finds peace in the pure calmness of infinity. The joy he experienced on Earth is transitory while that of the liberated self is everlasting. In his view, immortality is the reward for doing good, as at last the true self encounters the new experience of dwelling within God.

The second phase of life, he believed, is one without a physical body in which there is no suffering, pain or death. Finally, he came to believe that anyone who seeks knowledge about God and lives a righteous life could become an enlightened person, capable of revealing divine knowledge.

*   *   *

After this enlightening experience, Matthew opened his eyes and looked around. He felt strangely elated. With his mind clear, he decided to return to the village of Sutton. His desire was to share the knowledge he had found with others and to restore the relationship he once had with Rebecca and her mother.

On his way to the widow's home, he noticed a shady tree where Dusty Mills used to meditate frequently. Feeling tired after hours of walking, he decided to rest under that tree. It was a windy day, and because of the strong winds, dry leaves of the tree were falling to the ground. It became difficult for him to sleep peacefully because some leaves occasionally fell on his face. While lying beneath the tree, he began to smell a sweet fragrance. Believing that someone else was nearby, he got up and anxiously looked around. He saw no one and this made him wipe his eyes in doubt. Seconds later, the sweet scent changed into an awful smell of a decaying corpse. It was such an unbearable stench that he quickly placed the palm of his hand over his nostrils to block it. Unable to restrain his breathing, he gagged a few times and then spat on the ground.

Matthew became bewildered by this mysterious odor and began moving the dead leaves on the ground with his feet in an effort to find out what was causing it. As he slowly walked around the tree he sensed the presence of someone close to him. Still unable to see anyone, he quivered with fear. Briefly, he felt cold and got the weird feeling that someone was restraining him from moving. Slowly, the hairs on his arms stood on end while he scratched his head in total perplexity.

In the midst of this frightening experience, an enlightened Matthew managed to keep his composure. He quickly reflected upon the knowledge he had gained in conscientious contemplation regarding the subject of the mind taking a longer time to die than the flesh. He realized that since, when Dusty was alive this tree used to be his favorite place to meditate and rest. He came to believe that this strange presence was Dusty Mills' whose thoughts had not yet been erased. In a strong and commanding voice he cried: "Dusty, you are dead! Stop identifying yourself with the physical body or things of the Earth. Accept death and allow your thoughts to enter a state of tranquillity."

Upon uttering these words, Matthew could no longer sense the presence or smell anything putrid. He then realized that there was no reason for him to fear the unknown because it was powerless. He believed that the longer the true self keeps identifying itself with earthly things, the longer it remains an unseen force that wanders.

This strange encounter with what he termed "the unknown" was something new to him. The enlightened Matthew showed no fear as he lay to slumber under the same tree. He believed that, by hearing those strong words, Dusty Mills had finally accepted death. The knowledge he gained in conscientious contemplation assisted him to analyze things in a rational way. After a few hours he woke up from a peaceful sleep and continued on his journey to Sutton.

At the widow's home, Matthew was surprised to see no one. Eager to meet her and her daughter, Rebecca, he began to inquire about their whereabouts. He learned that after he had departed, the frustrated widow abandoned her child and secretly went away to another part of the country. Rebecca had been taken to a nearby foster home which had been recently built for the homeless.

The unfortunate situation of the widow and her child made Matthew feel guilty. Eager to meet Rebecca, he immediately went to the foster home. This shelter for the homeless was owned and maintained by a middle-aged couple who devoted their time to serving the needs of humanity. When he arrived at the home, Rebecca was delighted to see him. She believed her father had returned to her once more. Rebecca hugged him tightly and he became deeply touched. Her gentle smile was captivating and the way she rested her head on his shoulders showed she was yearning for parental affection.

His request to gain custody of the child was turned down by the couple as they were unsure whether to trust him or not, having heard about the earlier circumstances. Matthew, disappointed, realized that he had lost the trust of others. However, being enlightened, he was quick to understand the feelings of those who judged him harshly. In spite of being rejected, he showed no signs of animosity towards anyone. Instead, he complimented the couple for their good work in taking care of the homeless children. Realizing how dedicated and patient they were in providing care for others, he thought to himself that they were probably religious people. He felt it would be beneficial to share with them the knowledge he had found in conscientious contemplation.

After a brief conversation with the couple, he was surprised to learn that they were not religious, so whatever he had to say about God was of little importance. The couple was agnostic and, regardless of their doubts that the existence of God is incapable of being known, strongly believed in the performance of selfless actions.

Reflecting upon the knowledge he had received in conscientious contemplation, he realized that with these acts of goodness, this couple was in a way bringing themselves closer to liberation. He felt convinced that there must be more than one righteous path to heal the human mind, and the path was the choice of each individual.

In the years to follow, Matthew became popular among other sages who realized that whatever he said was inspirational and full of wisdom. In time, even the agnostic couple realized that he was indeed a learned man, and gradually they too began to have a clearer understanding of God. He became the follower of a path to God called Conscientious Contemplation. In spite of having a different ideology from other spiritual aspirants, he greatly respected the religious beliefs of others. He embraced all faiths with an open mind and strongly believed that there were many paths to God. In various places of worship, he felt comfortable listening to others from different religious beliefs glorify the name of God. Matthew felt that he should not be unyielding or fanatical about what he believed in, for as his mind continued to develop, his beliefs might change and he might become ever more enlightened. He strongly felt that human beings in prayer have a common objective in wanting to identify themselves with that Single Source called God.

NOTES

NOTES

NOTES

About the Author

Jagdish R. Singh was born on June 29, 1953 in the town of Blenheim on the island of Leguan, Guyana. In 1977, he immigrated to Canada where he later studied spiritual beliefs and ancient mythology. Since then he has been actively writing adult fiction and children stories.

Printed in the United States
2946

9 780595 191970